martinis & musicians

katrina marie

Don't let fear rule your life. Sometimes the things that scare you the most are the things worth going after.

author's note

This book contains subjects that might be triggering. The following are included:

- Child abandonment (Mentioned not shown)

If you want to see the content warnings of all my books, you can find it on my website.

prologue

WELCOME TO ASHEVILLE. That sign has never been more beautiful than it is right now. My headlights spotlighting it in the fading sun. Never in a million years did I think I would be back here. At least, not with any intention of staying. But I've missed this town. The way everyone feels like family... even if they don't really know you. That sort of feeling isn't something I've ever been used to.

The ticket to the event happening at Out of the Ashes for New Year's Eve is sitting on the seat beside me. I'm not sure what they have on the agenda, but I need to be there. It's a sign of how much has changed since I left. The stage was barely under construction back then. Now they are holding events. And not just that, but ticketed events. The bar seems to have grown so much, and I hate I haven't been a part of it.

Hell, I wouldn't have known about it if they didn't have a social media presence, which is also new. They would have turned me away at the door without a ticket. It won't be my first stop, though. I need to check into my room and get ready.

My foot lifts off the gas pedal as I come into downtown. The speed limit drops drastically, and I really don't need to get a ticket on my first night in town. That won't bode well for what I hope to be my grand return.

The parking lot at the bar is full as I pass by, and I wonder if I should forego stopping at the hotel. The FOMO is hitting hard, but I've been in the car for hours, and I really need the time to decompress before I stop by and see everyone.

Staying my course, I leave Out of the Ashes behind me. They'll be there when I get back. If I know Angie and Carlos, it'll be all hands on deck tonight. It's also where everyone who wants to be a part of the celebration will be. Hopefully I'll see some people that don't work there.

The hotel is a couple of blocks up, and I pull into the parking lot. There isn't a driveway to pull into before checking in, so I park my car in the closest space I can find. Grabbing my bags out of the backseat, I lug it to the lobby. An older lady I've never seen before is sitting at the front desk. "Hello, dear. How can I help you?"

"Hi," I wave, "I have a reservation for Lisa Cole."

The woman hunts and pecks at the keyboard for a few minutes before finding my name. "Ah, yes. Lucky for you, we had a cancellation when you booked. The event happening at Angie's bar has filled up most of the hotels in town." As if I didn't already realize that when I tried to book at the other ones. She pauses for a few minutes, checking my details. "I have you down for three nights."

"Yes, ma'am." I just hope that's long enough to find a living situation. Maybe Delilah will have pity on me and let me crash at her house for a couple of days. Or until I get back on my feet. That's if she hasn't gotten wind of my betrayal and will take me in. I'm hoping like hell Angie and Carlos will give me my job back. I loved working there, and I'd like to continue that. As soon as I get steady work, I can find a place of my own.

Finally, the woman's name tag is visible. Vicky works on

getting a key ready for me and asks me to swipe my card. As soon as I do, and I've signed the agreement, she hands me the key. "Here you go. There's free breakfast in the mornings, and check out when you leave is at eleven."

"Thank you so much, Vicky." I grab my bags again and head toward the elevators. There are only five floors, and my room is on the third. I haul my things into the elevator and wait until it hits my floor. Once the doors open, I step out and make a note of the direction of my room. Turning to the right, I follow the hall to the last room on the left.

As soon as I'm in, I take two steps and drop my bags on the floor. Finally, a space bigger than my car. I glance at the clock and decide I have time to lie down for a bit. A little cat nap before getting ready will do my body good. Hopefully, everyone else will be as happy to see me as I am to see them. Only time will tell, and I'll worry about that in a few hours.

I flop on the bed, and push a pillow under my head. For now, sleep is all that matters.

* * *

I rush to the door at Out of the Ashes. My alarm didn't go off, and I'm getting here with little time to spare before midnight. Rushed is not how I planned to enter the bar, but here we are. My hand pounds on the locked door. This is a first. The door has never been locked. A person who I assume works here comes to the door. "I need to get inside, please."

"I'm sorry. It's a ticketed event."

I pull the piece of paper out of my back pocket. "I have mine right here. I'm so sorry. I didn't mean to get here so late."

"Okay. Stop by the bar and grab your drink." He opens the door wider. "Enjoy the rest of the show."

The inside looks the same, but different. Besides the music coming from the stage area, there are decorations all over the rest of the bar. Christmas trees are tucked into corners, and mistletoe hangs from entryways. There are even small bulb lights against the edge of the bar. This never happened when I worked here. If I had to guess, this was all Stella's idea. It's not a bad one considering it gives the space a photographic aesthetic. I'm just surprised Angie said okay. Or, better yet, Carlos. He doesn't seem the type to go all out for holidays.

My eyes widen as soon as I see Delilah and my feet carry me toward her. "Lilah, it's been forever."

"Lisa!" she screams and throws her arms around me. "What are you doing here?"

There's a guy standing next to her, but until she introduces him, I won't say anything. "I'm back. For good this time."

"You sure about that?" It feels good to have my best friend teasing me once again. Even if I'm not sure I deserve it.

"Definitely. The world out there doesn't hold the family I have here," I notice the stage and gasp, "it's finally finished. And...Devin is playing?" I mean, clearly, he's on the stage, but it comes out like a question, anyway.

"Yeah, he's opening for the next act." Delilah grins while looking at the stage. No doubt proud of her brother for realizing his dream. "How did you get in?"

"I bought a ticket. I didn't know it was going to be a concert. I thought it was just a party." When Lilah turns toward the bar, I let my gaze linger on the stage at what could have been.

"Lucky you. It's the first sold out show of the year. I imagine there will be many more." She grabs one flute of champagne and hands it to me. "We're about to do the midnight toast if you want to hang out."

I look between the two of them and smirk. "I'll just go over there." I wink before joining the crowd. As much as I'd love to toast with her, I'm worried she'll see how my eyes stay on her brother a little too long.

I don't go to the front of the stage. He doesn't know I'm back, and I want to keep it that way for as long as I can.

As soon as I'm settled between a group of people, he stops the music and starts the countdown. Five. Four. Three. Two. One. I lift my glass into the air and toast to a year of smarter choices. At least, I hope it will be. I don't want to leave this town again because I fucked up.

He starts singing again, finishing up his song, and I make my exit. I'll see everyone else tomorrow. Right now...I need to get away from temptation.

Because if there is one person who can break my will, it's Devin.

1
lisa

MY OLD ROOM is exactly the same. Down to the things I had on the dresser. Even some clothes I left behind are in the closet. Delilah always expected me to come back. It should feel me with joy or gratitude, but it doesn't. It feels as bad as the guilt I carry with me.

As much as I want to be in a place of my own, I couldn't stay at the hotel anymore. The lack of space was an issue, but so was my dwindling bank account. I only have so much money to carry me over until I find a job.

Calling Delilah was the only option left. She took me in, no questions asked. Which is why I'm standing in awe of my untouched room. She should have rented it out. Though I'm grateful she didn't. Otherwise, I wouldn't have a place to stay right now.

"Do you need help bringing anything inside?" The sound of her voice startles me. "Bryce should be here in a bit, and he can grab whatever you need on his way in."

"No," I shake my head, still taking in my room. "I've got everything right here." I point toward my suitcase and bags sitting on top. Traveling light is something I've learned over the years. I can't get attached to a location if I'm able to leave at a moment's notice.

Except that isn't exactly true. I'm back in Asheville. A small part of me knew I'd make this my home. Even if I don't want to admit it.

"Oh, okay." She backs away. "I'll let you get settled in. If you need anything, we'll be out here watching movies."

"Thanks." I feel awful for intruding on her time with her boyfriend. For being the blip in their routine. I'm sure this isn't exactly what she expected when she saw me at the bar on New Year's Eve. Before she heads out, I ask, "Is he here a lot? I'm not cramping your style or anything, right?"

"Not at all." She waves my question away. "He has me hooked on cheesy movies, and that's what we spend my days off doing. We sometimes go to his house, but I feel awkward over there. His mom is nice, but being cuddled up with her son while she's in the next room feels weird."

"Wow," I laugh. "He's really gotten under your skin. But I completely understand about the whole Mom thing. That would probably weird me out, too."

"Yeah, but totally worth it. Are you going to talk to Angie about getting your job back at the bar?"

"That's the plan. As long as they'll have me." I hope like hell Angie lets me work there again. That place is even more so my home than this house with Delilah.

"I don't think you have to worry about that." She rushes toward me and gives me a quick hug. "They were upset you didn't stay after the show. All you have to do is talk to Angie and Carlos. Who knows...they may even find a better position for you."

Huh, I wonder what makes her say that. I know Carlos is the co-owner. But what other spot would I work well in that isn't guiding people to their tables, or helping out where needed?

"I know. It just feels weird after being gone for so long." It was barely six months. But so much has changed, and I feel like an outsider. The new girl in town, even though I know everyone. And most everyone knows me. At least, the regulars at the bar did before I packed my bags and hauled ass out of town.

"You know, you never told me why you were leaving. I hope it wasn't something I did."

Talk about a punch to the gut. I need to tell her. She deserves to know, especially since she thinks it's her fault. If I wasn't such a coward, I would have told her before I left town. But I didn't. Now's my chance.

"No, it wasn't you at all. It was be—"

I'm interrupted by a knock on the door and a guy's voice calling, "Del?"

Saved by her boyfriend. I'll tell her about me and Devin...eventually. Maybe. "Crap, he's here early. Let me know if you need help with anything. Or you can come out there and watch movies with us."

"Sure thing. I'll join y'all after I finish putting my things away."

"Okay." My best friend practically skips out of my room to the man who has captured her heart. I'm happy for her. She deserves all the love in the world. And she's going to need someone to lean on when she finds out I betrayed her one rule all those months ago.

I set my duffle bag and backpack on the bed before unzipping them. One by one, I place the items on the bed. I need to take stock of what I have.

It's mostly trinkets from the cities I've visited. Hopping from metroplex to metroplex all around Texas. I even stayed in Louisiana for a bit. That's definitely a place I want to go on a girl's trip. But I never stay long enough to build relationships.

The dresser is the only place I can think of to hold the

mementos. The only space where they'll be on display. Now that those are out of the way, I place my brush, makeup, and other toiletries in a drawer.

As much as I loved visiting other areas, I did miss having a place to call home. Somewhere I feel safe and loved. It's the whole reason I came back, to be around the family I formed for myself.

My phone dings with a message as I'm opening my suitcase. There's only one of two people it can be.

Lifting the phone, I glance at the screen. Huh. That's not who I thought it would be. My money was on Devin or Angie. Because I know he has to know I'm back by now.

CARLOS

So, you're just going to act like we don't exist. Is that it?

I don't know how to respond to that. Either way, he'll be upset. None of them were a fan of me leaving, but I didn't think they'd make such a big deal about me coming back.

LISA

Why on earth do you think that?

CARLOS

You came to the New Year's event and didn't say a word to me or Angie.

LISA

I was waiting until I got settled. I'm coming by the bar tonight.

CARLOS

You better.

Well, it's good to know he's still bossy as hell. At least that hasn't changed. There's no getting out of stopping at the bar tonight. One of them is likely to send out a search party. Not that it'll be hard. They know where Delilah lives.

Tossing my phone on the bed, I open my suitcase and pull out the clothes. The TV from the living room is loud through the thin walls. Drowning it out, I get back to work. It doesn't take me long to put everything where it goes, and I sigh in relief once it's done.

A part of me wants to hide out in here until I decide to go to Out of the Ashes. But I know Delilah will eventually come looking for me.

I walk out of my room, down the hall, into the living room. Delilah and Bryce are snuggled up on the sofa, but they aren't just watching a movie. No, they are making out.

A squeak escapes my lips and they jump apart like two teens caught by their parents. Delilah's cheeks turn pink, and she hides behind her hand. "When did you become so quiet when you walk? I didn't even hear you."

"I didn't, but it's okay." And it is, she deserves this bit of happiness and alone time. I also know I don't exactly want to be around them making out. It's just not my cup of tea.

"Come watch this movie with us."

"I'm good." I glance at the screen. "I've already seen this one." Luckily, I have, so it's not a lie. As much I didn't want to lie to her again, I would have told a tiny one to get out of staying here right this second.

"Are you sure? We can pick something else."

"Yeah." I clasp my hands together in front of me before jerking my thumb over my shoulder. "Carlos actually texted me. I'm supposed to stop by the bar."

She grins. "I wondered how long that would take."

"Not long." Though I'm surprised it wasn't sooner.

Bryce has his eyes on anything but me. No doubt he's embarrassed. He shouldn't be, though. I'm the one who barged into their lives and messed up their routine.

"Do you want us to go with you?"

"No, no." I wave my hands. "I'm a big girl and perfectly capable of going on my own."

"Okay." Concern is written all over her face, and I need to get out of here ASAP. "If you change your mind, let me know."

"Will do." Things feel awkward with Delilah, and it's my fault. "I'm just going to, uh, get ready. I can't walk in there looking like this."

Before my friend says anything else, I hightail it back to my room. Out of the Ashes will be a good distraction. For now, at least.

* * *

It's still weird coming to Out of the Ashes as a regular patron and not someone who works here. There's also no line wrapped around the building. I bet Delilah is happy she doesn't have to deal with the folks who were unhappy about the wait to get in. But there was nothing we could do back then. We didn't want to break fire code.

The music is loud as I open the door. It's not live music, though. It's pumping through the speakers. I guess live music only happens on the weekends. It makes sense. That's when the bar is busiest.

The person standing behind the host stand is new. I've never seen them before, and I'm glad Delilah isn't working every night the same way I was. The bar was growing faster than we could keep up. It's nice knowing Angie and Carlos have a team behind them to make it an enjoyable work experience.

"Hi, can I lead you to a table?"

"No, I'm fine. I'll sit at the bar."

"It's open seating. Help yourself." She waves toward the bar.

"Thanks."

Luckily there are open seats close to the door. I want a quick escape plan just in case I chicken out and leave before I see anyone. This is a newish feeling for me. When I left home at eighteen, I swore to myself I'd never let anyone make me feel like a disappoint. But this is the other way around. I'm terrified of disappointing these people who mean so much to me.

A tall guy with short hair rushes toward me from the other side of the bar. He must be new as well. "What's your poison?"

He leans against the bar and lifts a corner of his mouth into a smirk. He's attractive, and he knows it. That's a dangerous combination, and I think he's trying to gauge my interest. I glimpsed him on New Year's Eve, but I didn't engage with him at all. Once I realized Devin was on the stage, he had my full attention.

"Cut it out with the flirting, Eric." Carlos's voice is loud enough to be heard over the music as he makes his way toward me. So much for attempting to sneak out before anyone saw me. It's shitty, I know. But I'm doing my best to not feel like a complete outsider with all the new people in this place where I practically lived. "She's not interested."

"How do you know?" Eric glances toward Carlos. "She hasn't even spoken yet."

"He's not wrong." I shrug my shoulders. "And I'd like a martini, please."

Carlos lifts an eyebrow. "Since when do you like those? You've always had margaritas."

"I'm allowed to like other drinks." Rolling my eyes, I get out of my seat and wrap my arms around Carlos's waist. "It's good to see you. I've missed y'all so much."

"Are you sure?" He chuckles and I forgot how much I've

missed this man who has always been like an older brother to me.

I pull back from him. "Yeah, why?"

"Because you haven't been around for half a year. And...there wasn't so much as a call."

He's not even that much older than me and he's doing the whole protective parent thing. Not only that, it seems to be sharpened. Like he grew up and has new responsibilities. What happened while I was gone?

"Sorry. I didn't mean to fall off the face of the earth. I just needed some space." I take a deep breath and sit back down on the stool. I also knew if I talked to anyone here, other than my infrequent texts to Delilah, I'd come back sooner than I was ready.

He says nothing else, just slides onto the stool next to me. Giving me those moments to gather my thoughts.

The bartender, Eric, slides my drink in front of me and hands Carlos a bottle of water. "Thanks," I mutter. "Any chance you know of rentals available?"

"Why do you need a rental? I figured you'd be staying with Delilah again."

How do I say this without seeming ungrateful? "I am staying with her, but it's not the same as before. I walked in on her and Bryce making out. I don't want to cramp her style." And I really don't want to accidentally see anything happen. "She has her own thing going on, and it's not fair of me to barge into it."

"You can stay with me." Eric is pouring a drink for a customer, and leaning against the bar. He's pretty good at the whole multi-tasking thing.

"How?" Carlos tilts his head to the side. "You don't even know each other?"

"And?" Eric scoffs. "We can get to know each other."

"I'm not dating you." He's needs to know that upfront

before he gets any ideas in his head. I didn't come back to Asheville to jump into a relationship.

"I got the message," he holds up his hands, "but you need a place to stay, and I have an empty room. You'd just have to pay our man here the other half of the rent."

A lot really has changed if Carlos is renting out his house. I need to ask Delilah for all the details on what has happened in the last six months.

"Or you can stay with me." My entire body stiffens at the sound of his voice. I knew I'd run into him eventually. What I didn't expect was for him to invite me to stay with him in front of my friends and former coworkers. What the hell is he thinking?

2
devin

THIS IS A HAPPY SURPRISE. Delilah told me Lisa was back in town. That she was here to stay. A small part of me hopes I'm the reason. I handled things badly the first time around, and I want another shot. But based on her reaction...that will not be as easy as I hoped.

It took me a second to realize what they were talking about. I wasn't trying to eavesdrop, but it was hard since they are seated in the chairs directly in front of the door. My only purpose today was to talk to Angie and make sure I'm good to perform this weekend.

I wasn't expecting to see the one I let slip away sitting in front of me, looking for a place to live. The question slipped out of my mouth before I even realized it.

Her back stiffens, and she doesn't budge. Eric and Carlos turn toward me. Carlos with his brows raised, and Eric with mistrust written all over his face. I don't blame him; he doesn't really know me. And as far as I know, Carlos knows nothing about the relationship Lisa and I hid from everyone.

"No offense, Devin, but you don't exactly have room for her either." Carlos isn't delivering a jab, just a statement that he knows to be true. I have what amounts to a tiny home beside my parents' house. It has one bedroom, and instruments cluttering up the space.

Honestly, I don't know how we didn't get caught dating when she was here. It's not like my parents couldn't look out their window and see her car parked by my house. Or, maybe they did, and decided not to say anything. Who knows...

"You're right." I nod in agreement. "But if it's short term, we could work something out."

I'm waiting for Lisa to turn around. To acknowledge my existence, but she's not making a move. I've definitely fucked up before I've had time to fix things between us.

Finally, she turns around. "Thanks for the offer, but I think rooming with Eric may be better. I'll have my own space. Besides, I wouldn't want to disturb your writing process."

Great, that's what she thinks is going to happen. I've written some of my best songs when she was at my place. She's my muse, and she doesn't realize it.

I can argue my point or let it rest. It could work in my favor, but Lisa is stubborn. Once she's decided something, that's it.

"Well, if you change your mind, you know where to find me." I don't want her to stay with Eric. He's flirty and it's only a matter of time before she falls for his charm. I turn toward Carlos, "Is Angie in the office?"

"Yep." He nods in the direction of the hall before taking a sip of water. "Just knock before you go in. She's not getting along well with the computer and I think she's ready to chunk it."

"Will do." I glance at Lisa one last time before heading toward the office, hoping she'll say something else. But she doesn't.

Angie is stabbing at her keyboard when I knock on the open door, muttering something under her breath. She doesn't realize I'm there, and I knock again. Still nothing. "Angie," I call out as I knock for the third time.

She jumps back in her chair and almost topples backward before regaining her balance. "You scared the hell out of me, Devin."

"Sorry," I hold my hands up in surrender. "I knocked a couple of times, but you didn't answer."

"It's fine. I need to take a break from this, anyway." She stands and comes around the front of the desk. "What can I do for you?"

I step inside the office and make my way toward her. "I just wanted to double check my performance schedule and make sure everything is good with it."

"As of right now, yes." She glances at her desk behind her. "Stella is looking for more acts to book. I think she's trying to get Crooked Halo to come back in the next few months if their touring schedule allows it. But the weekends are wide open right now."

"Awesome." Crooked Halo coming back will do great things for the bar since they are an upcoming act. One day I hope to have as many people filling the crowd as they do. "I can keep an eye out for other bands if she wants some help."

"Really?" She stares at me in disbelief. "I figured you'd want the monopoly on playing time."

She's wrong. I'm not that kind of person. Well, not completely. "I do like having the stage whenever I want it, but the more bands that play here, the more people come in. And that's good business for both of us."

Not to mention if more acts come in here, especially bigger ones, people in the music industry will take notice. It's a chance for me to get a break. To make it big doing something I always treated like a hobby, but want to make my career. Being an artist isn't easy.

"You have a point." Angie nods. "I'll let Stella know you want to help."

"Thanks, Ang." I point over my shoulder. "I'm gonna head out. I'll see you tomorrow night?"

"You'll probably see Carlos or Eric. I'm off that night."

"Cool." I turn toward the door and take a step. "Oh, Lisa is up front in case you didn't know."

"Really?"

"Yep. I saw her when I walked in."

She rushes past me and yells over her shoulder, "Close the door on your way out."

Wow. It looks like I'm not the only one Lisa didn't see when she got back into town. Apparently, my sister is the only one she cares about enough to see. I push that hurt down. This isn't about me. I'm sure Lisa has her reasons for being back.

I follow Angie at a slower pace and close the door behind me. Slowly, I walk back into the bar, doing my best to avoid the area Lisa is in.

It's hard seeing her here and knowing she isn't going to make time for me the way she used to.

Angie has Lisa in a bear hug as I walk past them. I wave to nobody in particular as I exit the bar. Hell, I don't even think anyone saw me. But that's fine. Lisa is happy and here.

A gust of wind blows through the parking lot and I shove my hands in my pocket. The sky is opposite of how it was when I walked into the bar. The bright shine of the sun is gone as dark gray clouds move in. The weather perfectly matching my mood now.

I could stay and drink for a bit, try to get Lisa to actually talk to me. But I won't. My feet move toward my car. There's only one thing I want to do right now, and that's write my feelings.

* * *

The rain is beating down on the roof of my house, and the words aren't coming. I thought for sure I'd have something to write about. Lyrics to put down on the page to play this weekend at the bar.

People aren't going to pay attention to what I'm playing if I don't have anything new. It gets repetitive. I could play covers of songs. While that's fun, I'd much rather play my own music.

I need something to materialize on the paper in front of me. Instead, scratched out words are scattered on the page. Is it because of my interaction with Lisa earlier? I don't know, but I need to figure it out.

There's a knock on the door and I don't bother asking who it is. Instead, I yell "come in" to be heard over the storm.

I throw my pen across the table and close my notebook. It's clear I won't have any good ideas tonight.

The door opens and for split second, I let myself hope it's Lisa, but that's squashed when my dad walks in. He's carrying a plate covered in foil in one hand, and an umbrella in the other.

"Hey, Dad." I stand, grabbing the plate for him so he can close his umbrella. I'd like to say I don't believe in bad luck, but tonight is not the night to tempt the fates.

He closes the door and sets the umbrella on the floor beside the door. "Your mom asked me to bring you what we had for dinner." He pulls the only other chair out at my table and takes a seat. "I guess the writing isn't going well?"

"How can you tell?" Sometimes it's like he has a sixth sense about my creativity. It's kind of freaky.

"Well, your pen is on the floor and your notebook is closed. It's rare I ever see that. Even when you aren't actively working on a song, it's always open."

"Yeah, things aren't going great." I sigh before sitting down. "I was hoping to have something new before I perform at Out of the Ashes this weekend, but it doesn't look like that's going to happen."

He taps his knuckles on the table a few times. I don't think he's going to give any input, but finally he speaks. "I think it'll all work out in the end. You'll find your inspiration and be able to write when the time is right. But I wonder if this has something to do with a certain girl who's come back."

No way. There's no way he actually knows what happened. "Why would Lisa have anything to do with it?"

"Son," he shakes his head. "I'm not dumb, and you aren't as sneaky as you thought you were."

"What do you mean?"

"You realize this is right next to the house, right? We can see who comes and goes. Her car was over here a lot considering Delilah doesn't live here."

Damn it. "You can't tell Delilah. She would be pissed."

He throws his hands up, "You have nothing to worry about there. This is between you, Lisa, and your sister. We aren't getting in the middle of it. You can deal with that on your own."

"Thank you," I whisper. "But you might be right to some extent. I saw her today."

"Where?"

"At the bar. I wanted to talk to Angie, and she was sitting at the bar talking to Carlos and Eric. She's looking for another place to stay."

"Why?" Dad's eyebrows scrunch together. "Isn't she staying with your sister?"

Nodding, I pull the plate toward me and lift off the foil. "I don't know all the details. I walked in at the end of the conversation. And I may have said she could stay here."

"Devin," he scolds me. It's the tone of voice I was always

terrified of when I was younger. It meant I was in big trouble. "You can't think that's a good idea. Especially when you were sneaking your relationship with her behind Delilah's back."

"Yeah, I know." I put the foil back on the plate. I'll eat when he leaves. "I don't know what came over me. I heard Eric offer her his extra room, and it came out."

"Looks like you aren't over her, Son." He scoots his chair back and stands. "You're old enough to make your own decisions, but tread carefully. You know your sister doesn't like you dating her friends. If you and Lisa want to make something of this, you need to talk to Delilah."

He doesn't say anything else, grabs his umbrella, and walks out the front door. Ugh, parents can be so frustrating. It's solid advice. Something I already know I should do, but I seriously doubt Lisa is going to give me the time of day again.

Standing, I move to pick up the pen I didn't realize fell on the floor, and set it back on the table.

Two steps and I'm at the kitchen counter. The drawer sticks as I pull it open to get a fork. I should probably fix that, but that's a problem for another day.

Fork in hand, I sit down, take the foil off the plate again and take a bite of the broccoli. Mom must have sensed I would need comfort food tonight. Parents, they know you better than you know yourself sometimes.

As I'm eating, I think about what my dad said. He wasn't wrong. I'm not over Lisa. It's possible I never will be. She's the first woman I ever really cared about, and I royally screwed that up.

I still remember the first day I met her. She was new to town and answered the advertisement my sister put out for a roommate. Delilah wanted me there to make sure the person wasn't a serial killer.

Lisa definitely wasn't that. She ended up becoming my sister's best friend. Her bubbly personality and love of life are what drew me to her. Even though my sister and I hung out a lot, I found even more reasons to be around them. To be around Lisa until it eventually turned into more.

And I ruined it. Words flood my brain and I push my plate away. I open my notebook and turn to the next empty page. My hand flies across the paper. The inspiration I couldn't find earlier hits me full force and I don't want to lose them.

3
lisa

IT'S ALWAYS weird to see Out of the Ashes without cars in the parking lot. It makes sense because it's closed, but it's still weird.

When I woke up this morning, I had a text from Angie on my phone telling me to meet her here. So here I stand. The locked door between me and Angie.

Raising a hand, I tap against the glass. The sound is barely audible. There's no way Angie heard it in the back. Deep down, I'm scared they won't take me back. Worried I'll disappoint them if they do.

I turn around, one foot in the air to step off the sidewalk. The lock behind me clicks, and I pause. How did they hear that?

"Where are you going?" Carlos says.

Of course, it would be both of them wanting to see me. Maybe he was in the front waiting for me. Setting my foot down, I spin toward him. "Nowhere."

"You sure about that?" He pushes the door until it's completely open. "Come on. It isn't bad, I promise."

"Okay." This unsettling fear is new to me. After I left

home, I promised myself I wouldn't be scared of anything. I'd tackle whatever life had to throw at me. But coming back to a town I left behind? To people I care about? That's terrifying. It's why I never went back to anyone.

I follow Carlos inside. He waits until I've passed him before closing and locking the door behind us. I stand by the hostess stand, unsure of where he wants me to go.

"Angie has donuts where we do our staff meetings." He points toward the main dining area. "I'll grab us some water and meet you over there."

They know I can't resist donuts, and I'm certain they are going to give me my job back if they are bringing those.

"Hey Lisa," she gets up and gives me a hug, "take a seat."

I pull out the seat closest to her and sit down. After I pull a donut out of the box, I take a bite. These have got to be my favorite donuts ever. Aside from my friends, I think I missed these the most.

Carlos sits down opposite of us. "We know you're just getting settled, but we wanted to talk to you about your old job."

Talk about getting down to business. He's not wasting any time. At least, I don't have to grovel for my job like I thought I would need to do. "I can have my job back?"

"Yes..." Angie begins.

"And no," Carlos finishes.

"What do you mean?" This seems pretty cut and dry to me. Either I get my job back or I don't. Curiosity courses through me. They have to have a reason for being so obscure.

Angie nods toward Carlos for him to explain. "We'd like to take you back on as one of the hosts. For now, anyway."

Because that doesn't sound foreboding. "Does that mean I need to continue my search for a job?"

"Not at all." Angie sits up straighter and takes another

donut. "We want to put you through bartending school so you can manage the bartenders."

What the hell? When have I ever given them the idea that I'm bartender material? "Isn't that Carlos's job?"

"I'm actually trying to cut back some of those responsibilities and help Angie with the day-to-day stuff."

That doesn't sound like the Carlos I used to work with at all. He basically lived at this bar. "Why the change? You used to be a workaholic."

"That's what having a family does to you."

"What?" That was quick. And there's only one person who could manage to pull him out of working so much.

"Delilah didn't tell you?"

"Tell me you have a family now? No." I knew I should have gotten her to give me updates. When I would text, or call, to check in, I made sure to steer away any conversation about the people here. It hurt too much thinking about everyone getting on with their lives without me. Even though I'm the one who chose to leave.

"Do you remember that girl that came in with her friends all the time?"

"The one you were too scared to talk to?"

"Yeah, she's the one." Angie grins before grabbing her drink off the table. "Eric basically double dog dared him to ask her out. It was a whole thing."

"Yeah, yeah," he waves his hand in the air, "anyway, I want to make more time for her and her son, David."

"So, what's it like to be a family man?" As logical as it is, it's not something I've ever considered Carlos once again. I mean, I've seen him interact with his sisters and his mom and his great. But that's not the same as raising a kid. Especially one that isn't your own.

A huge smile forms on his face. "It's pretty amazing. David is such a great kid and shows a lot of promise in football."

Wow. He has the whole package. "Next thing you know; you'll be pulling up to the bar in a minivan."

His only response is a shrug. I feel like that's a considerable downplay of changes that might occur in his life. But who am I to judge? It's not his fault I have a terrible relationship with my mom. If this is what he wants, I'm happy for him.

"So," Carlos leans forward and sets his elbows on the table. "Is this something you might be interested in? If not, that's okay. But we want you back on the team."

It feels like a lot of responsibility. Am I ready for something like this? I've poured beer before, but I've never paid much attention to how other types of drinks are made. Big decisions aren't exactly my area of expertise.

Grabbing the bottle of water Carlos set in front of me, I open it and take a long drink. Anything to buy me some time. My old job is what I really wanted, but this opportunity...it wouldn't be smart to pass it up.

I set the bottle back on the table. "How soon would bartending classes start? And how will that interfere with my duties at the host stand?"

"Does that mean you're in?" Angie clasps her hands in her lap. "Honestly, I think you would make a killing as a bartender."

"Yes," I grin, "I'm in."

Will I be any good at it? Time will tell. But it's worth a shot. Besides, I'll be able to see all my favorite people. This is my first step in putting down roots in a town I love. With a community of people, I know will be there for me.

"Awesome," Angie claps, "when do you want to start?"

"Is tomorrow good?" I grab another donut and take a bite. "I need to let Delilah know I'm moving in with Eric, and I have a feeling there will be a long talk about that."

"Oh," Carlos furrows his brows, "you're actually going through with that?"

"Yep," another bite, "Delilah and Bryce need their space. Based on how much he seems to be over there, I have a feeling he'll be moving in sooner than later."

"Just be careful with Eric. He's a flirt and nosey as hell."

Angie laughs, and the sound fills the empty bar. "If he wasn't so nosey, you wouldn't be with Caroline. Give the kid a break. He's one of the good ones."

He holds up his hands. "I never said he was bad. But you know how he is."

Shaking my head, I giggle at the two of them arguing. You can tell they're not only business partners but friends. This is what I missed. Hanging out with my family, even if it's at work.

"He's harmless." I wave away Carlos's concern. "I think I made myself pretty clear last night that I wasn't interested. If it takes him more than that to get the hint, that's his problem. Not mine."

"True," he nods.

"I do need to know how much the rent is so I can pay my half. Also, is there a lease I need to add my name to?"

"Tell you want." Carlos claps his hands. "I'll have both of you meet me here, or at the house in the morning and we'll go over everything. Sound good?"

"Yep." I pull my phone out of my pocket and glance at the time. "Crap. I should probably get back. I didn't even let Delilah know I was leaving this morning. I don't want to freak her out."

She may be slightly younger than me, but that girl is a mother hen. Even when I left, she'd constantly send me messages checking in on me to make sure I was okay.

"Here," Angie puts the lid on the donuts. "Take these with you. I'm sure she'll appreciate breakfast."

"Are you sure?"

"Yep. We," she points between herself and Carlos, "don't need to eat all these."

"Speak for yourself." Carlos mutters.

"Okay," I pick up the box, "Carlos, I'll see you in the morning. Angie, see you tomorrow afternoon. If you need me to come in earlier, just text me."

"You got it."

Before they can say anything else, I rush toward the door. I'm not sure what I've done in my life to have such amazing people support me, but I'm not going to take it for granted.

* * *

Delilah's car is gone when I pull into the driveway. That's weird. She's an early bird, but I know for a fact she was still asleep when I left.

Once I'm parked, I grab the box of donuts and head inside. Honestly, I could take a cat nap. But I don't want to seem like an ungrateful house guest.

Setting the donuts on the table, I look for things to do. There are a few things out, and dishes in the sink. After washing those, I straighten up the blankets on the sofa. It's not like the house is a mess, but the small chores give me something to do.

She's still not back when I'm finished. I check my phone and don't have any messages from her. Maybe she and Bryce are doing something.

I grab the remote, and turn on the tv before lying down on the sofa. Shoving the closest pillow under my head, I find something to watch.

It's an old comfort movie of mine with fantasy and quests. I doubt most people my age have even seen it, but it's the one good thing my mom ever did for me. This movie has shown me the power of forging unlikely friendships and taking a chance on myself...even when life has other ideas.

"Lisa." I hear my name being called, and I jump up from the sofa. I can't believe I dozed off.

Delilah is standing just inside the door with Bryce behind her. He's carrying something, but I can't tell what it is. "Sorry. I didn't hear you come in."

"No worries." She holds up a bag. "We brought lunch. And..." She moves aside so her boyfriend can step beside her. "Cake!"

"Why do you have cake?" I shove my hair out of my face. "It's not my birthday."

"To celebrate you working at the bar again. Not to mention your promotion."

Word travels fast. "It barely happened a few hours ago. How do you already know?"

"Please," she waves my question away. "I knew before they even met with you this morning. They asked me if I thought you'd be interested."

That figures. Ugh, I forgot how uncomfortable it is sleeping on this sofa. My feet hit the ground with a thud and I stand, stretching my arms over my head.

"How did you know I'd say yes?"

"You like a challenge. I had no doubt you'd accept." She starts toward the small kitchen. "Now come eat lunch so we can cut into this cake."

She never ceases to amaze me. She makes the biggest deal out of the smallest things. I'm pretty sure this is something her parents did for her and Devin.

Jealousy slices through me. I never had that. Hell, I barely had any sort of acknowledgement for my birthday. I never knew my dad, and my mom treated me like a nuisance more than a child. But Delilah isn't my mom. She cares fiercely about her friends, and I'm lucky to call her one of mine.

I join them in the kitchen and pull out a chair. The cake is one that is already made in the store. You just grab it and go. It must be fate because it's my favorite, red velvet.

Bryce pulls containers out of the bag, checking the contents before setting it in front of us.

I pop open the container and my favorite pasta is inside. "Thank you both so much."

"Hold on," Bryce says. "That's not all."

He pulls a smaller container out of the bag and opens it before giving it to me. Its fries covered in cheese, bacon, and jalapeños. One of my all-time favorite appetizers. "You really didn't have to do all this."

"Nonsense," Delilah scoffs. "It's not every day your best friend comes home and gets a job. I want to do this for you."

She is the reason I have faith in people. "Thank you so much."

"Anytime." She takes a bite of her chicken strips. "So, when do you start?"

"Tomorrow afternoon." I say between bites. "I'll still be working the host stand, and filling in wherever they need me, until I'm certified to serve."

"Awesome. We'll at least be working together for a bit." She finishes her lunch and closes the container. "You better get your rest tonight."

"Why is that?" I know the bar was busy last night, but it wasn't anything I couldn't handle.

"Because it gets bananas when we have live music."

I almost forgot about that aspect. Curiosity pokes out its head about who the band will be. I'm not going to ask, though. Hopefully, it's a new artist I can get hooked on.

4
devin

THIS IS the first night I'll be performing at Out of the Ashes on a regular basis. If I'm being honest, I'm scared. I know most of the town showed up for the New Year's Eve bash. They applauded me and kept me going. But let's be honest, everyone was having a good time. I'm sure anyone would have gotten a standing ovation. Tonight, though...that could make or break how I continue this journey.

I park on the side of the building. Ideally, I'd walk through the front door. Not tonight. The back door in the alley is the direction my feet lead me. If the crowd in there hates me, I'll have a quick escape. Hopefully I won't need that. My hand on is on the handle, but it doesn't budge when I push it down. It's locked. Of course, it is. I'm not sure if this is Eric's idea of a joke, or if Angie forgot to let him know it needed to be unlocked. Either way...I'm not amused.

Setting my guitar case on the dirty pavement, I grab my phone from my back pocket. I unlock it and go directly to my messages. Maybe if I text Angie, she'll get this sorted out. My fingers hover over the screen. No. I'm not going to complain to her about this minor inconvenience. It's not like I'm some huge start and can demand things.

Let's be real, this is about me being scared to perform on my own for an entire night. Normally I have friends with me, playing their instruments, but they can't do Friday nights for various reasons. I can't fault them for that. It was my decision to play on my own tonight. And that is why I'm nervous. There aren't any drums or other guitars to back me up.

It's just me, my acoustic guitar, a stool, and a microphone. If I want to do this as a career, I need to get over myself and walk inside. I can do this.

Picking my guitar off the ground, I turn back toward the edge of the building. I can hear the music playing through the speakers inside the building. A part of me wonders if my music will be that loud with the amp.

Each footstep around the building brings me closer to the front door. To being alone on the stage. This is so much harder than playing football. I was in front of everyone in the stands, but their sole focus wasn't on me. Most of the time it was on Bryce. I was one of the teammates that helped get the ball down the field. This time...it's all me.

The glass door is in front of me. My reflection staring at me, daring me to grab the handle, knowing this is that do or die moment. Do I take the step and do what I've secretly dreamed of all my life. Yes. I grab the handle and pull.

The bar isn't exactly dark, but it has a subdued ambiance. It's not hyped up like most bars I've seen. Or even clubs, for that matter. It's one of the things I love about this place. The chill atmosphere. Let's just hope it's chill enough to not boo me off the stage despite how much they applauded me a couple of weeks ago.

"Devin?" The voice I've missed for so long catches my attention, and I stop in my tracks. What is she doing here? Not that it isn't a nice surprise, but I unexpected.

My eyes meet hers, and I smile. "Lisa, how are you?"

"Fine. Um, what are you doing here?" She looks confused to see me.

"I play tonight." A lump forms in my throat, hoping my nervousness doesn't show. After the way things went down with us before, I don't want her to see me as anything other than confident.

"Oh, okay." She looks everywhere but at me. "I guess you know where you need to go."

She shifts her focus to something on the stand. It's probably the layout of tables available. The small task dismissing me. But I need to make up for my behavior the other day.

"Hey." I reach out and touch her arm. She doesn't flinch, but her arm shifts out from under my fingers. Clearing my throat, I continue. If I don't, I'll chicken out, and prove to my dad that I'm not grown enough to own my mistakes. I pull my hand back and shove it in my pocket. "I'm sorry about butting into your conversation."

"What?" Her blond hair vibrates as she shakes her head.

"When you asking about a place to stay the other day. You were talking to Carlos and Eric." My eyes are focused on my feet because they look so much more interesting than the disdain that is probably in her eyes. "It was out of line. Especially given our history."

"Don't worry about it," she sighs, "it wasn't the place to insert yourself, but I appreciate the apology."

The bell above the door rings behind me, and I know it's time to move toward the backstage area. Even if I don't want to. Now, I look up. I need to make sure she's not just accepting the apology to get me out of her hair. "Maybe we can talk later?"

Her eyes are focused just above my shoulder at whoever just came in. Damn. She won't even look at me. "We'll see."

If I stay any longer, I'll be pressing my luck. Lisa is a very easy going, chill person until you wear out your welcome. I did that over six months ago, and I regret it every day. "Okay." I take a step forward. "I'll, uh, see you around."

So much for exuding confidence. That scenario also played out differently in my head. I knew she was mad about my comment, and I don't fault her for that. I should have kept my mouth shut. But the cool indifference from her is new. Something that was always saved for asshole customers who came in here and acted like jerks. Not me...never for me. It's further proof that I completely fucked up.

Maybe I don't deserve her forgiveness, or her time. Actually, I know I don't. Not after the way I reacted to one simple request she had when we were dating. The one thing I shouldn't have denied. But that's on me. All I can do going forward is see if she'll allow me to get close to her again. To give me another chance to prove I'm not a complete jackass.

Lingering around her isn't a good look, and I force my feet to move toward the back of the bar. Before I get set up, I need to double check some things with Carlos. I don't want to get up there and look stupid.

I also need to give myself time to get my bearings. Hope that talking to Lisa would energize me sinks to the pit of my stomach. If anything, it's made me more nervous than I was. Not only because she brushed me off, rightfully so, but also, I'll be performing and she'll hear me. Back when we were dating, she was my concert of one. My biggest supporter and fan, outside of my family. Now, I wonder if she'll realize how much of her, I've written into my songs.

"Aren't you supposed to be on stage in a few?" Carlos interrupts my thoughts.

Without even realizing it, I've made it to the office. It's like the people in the bar area were unnoticeable. I know it was crowded when I came in, but I must have unconsciously weaved my way through them.

"Yes. But I had a question I forgot to ask Angie the other day."

"Shoot." He leans against his desk and crosses his arms. He doesn't look happy to see me, and I'm guessing Lisa told him something about our past. Either that, or he somehow knows.

"How long do you want me to play?"

"What do you mean?"

"Well, some bars I've been to the band plays straight to closing time and others they stop about thirty minutes before." I glance down at my guitar case. "I just wanted to know which you prefer."

"I didn't know that." He shakes his head. "I guess that shows how long it's been since I've gone to another bar." He uncrosses his arms and stands up. "I guess it's up to you. You can play until we close or you can wrap it up earlier."

"Okay, sounds good. I'll get a feel for how the crowd is and decide while I'm up there."

"Do you need any help setting up?"

The sounds of people talking are getting louder with the increasing crowd. "No, thank you. As long as the setup is still the same from the party, I can do it."

"See you out there. Good luck, kid."

"Thanks." I wave him away and head toward the small backstage area. Repeating don't screw up with every step.

* * *

This...isn't so bad. I don't know why I was nervous. The crowd is great, and nobody has yelled boo once. A quick glance at my watch shows there to be about thirty minutes before the bar closes. Even though I still have a few more songs I can sing, I want some options for tomorrow night.

I take a drink of water from the bottle on the stool beside me. The chatter among the patrons is loud enough to give me that small break. Pulling the microphone off the stand, I clear my throat before speaking into it. "Is everyone having a good time tonight?"

The crowd offers up a boisterous yes in response. The elation flowing through my veins is more of an endorphin than I've ever felt. It's hard to describe and I hope like hell I get to feel this every time I step on stage.

"That's good to hear." I pause for dramatic effect. "Closing time is coming soon, and I have one last song for you. My name is Devin, and I hope you've enjoyed your night. Come back and see me."

I place the microphone back on the stand, sit on my stool and rest one foot on the step. Repositioning my guitar, I take a deep breath and strum the first note. Is it ballsy picking this as my last song? Absolutely. But I hope it will speak to Lisa. This was one of her favorite songs. It's a cover of a popular song and while I typically don't do them, I need her to know that I still think about her. It's a song about finding love and losing it. About wishing you still had it, and hoping like hell you can get it back.

It's a risky song to play for a closing not only because of what it's about, but because it's a ballad. Luckily nobody seems to mind. Some people are swaying at their tables, while others have grabbed their partners and are dancing. Their bodies close, feeling the rhythm and words flow through them. As much as I need Lisa to feel this performance, I'm glad the patrons are as well.

Leaning back the slightest bit, I glance toward the host stand. It's difficult to spot Lisa through the crowd of people and glass wall between the bar and dining area. Finally, I spot her. She's not beside the stand, but closer to the opening of the dining area. Visible, but just barely. Her eyes are focused on me, and when she catches me looking back at her, she turns away.

Well, that's good news. It means she's listening to the song I'm singing. Maybe she'll talk to me after the show. Hell, I'll even wait outside in the cold for her to get off. All I need is a chance.

The last words of the song leave my mouth and after a brief silence, applause fills the room. I set my guitar on the stand and get on my feet. "Thank y'all. I'll be back here tomorrow night with the rest of the band."

Considering this was my first time performing, and the fact it was an acoustic set, I think things went well. People start talking as I unplug my guitar and clear up my area. Out of the Ashes closes in about twenty minutes, and I don't want them cleaning up after me. While it might be a part of their job, I'm not that kind of person. I'm wrapping the cords when I feel someone behind me.

A part of me is worried it's Carlos, or Eric, here to give me a hard time. But Lisa's voice is what makes me turn around. "You did good tonight."

"Thanks." I'm not sure what else to say. A couple of seconds of silence fill the space between us. "So, how was my first performance you've seen?"

"It's not the first." She looks down and I can see her cheeks turn pink. The noise from the bar fades away. My sole focus is now on her.

"I don't think the performances at my house count," I laugh. Even though I loved those the most. After playing for her, we'd usually eat before peeling each other's clothes off.

She shakes her head before looking back at me. "I was here on New Year's Eve. I saw you open up for Crooked Halo. You were amazing then, but tonight was better."

Wait. What? How did I not notice her in the crowd? I've always been pretty in tune with her presence, and I doubt I would have missed her. "Where? I didn't see you."

"I stayed toward the back. It was the night I came back to

town." She shoves her hands in her back pockets, and I know it's one of her tells when she's nervous about what she's saying. "I also left before the other band came on."

"Why?" It's not like her to run away. Not normally, anyway. Though, I know I'm the reason. My screw up is what caused this tension between us.

"Because I wasn't really ready to see you, or talk to you, if you were going to be in the crowd afterward. It was easier if I left. Then I wouldn't have to face you, or your sister. I didn't want to ring in the new year with Delilah upset with me."

She has valid points, even if they are ones I don't want to hear. As much as I want to say something about it, this isn't the time or place. Not when there could be so many eyes watching. "What made tonight better?"

This time she looks away. I follow her gaze. People are paying their tabs and leaving the bar for the night. Farewells are being made, and I hope my question doesn't scare her off.

"It was all you." She lifts one hand to her face and taps her cheek, trying to find the words she wants to say without giving too much away. "More raw. It reminded me of all those nights I'd listen to you play. When you only had a handful of songs."

"That means a lot." That's all I can come up with. "It felt good being up here." Even if I'm pretty sure my hat has sweat soaking the band.

Rocking back and forth on her feet, she turns to leave the stage, but pauses for a split second. "If you still want to talk, we can. Just not here."

"I can wait for you in the parking lot." I give her a sly grin. "We can drive the back roads like we used to."

"I'll see you then." She walks off the stage and back to the front of the bar. Now I'm shaking in my boots. This time for entirely different reasons.

5
lisa

MY FEET CARRY me off the stage like someone is chasing me. In a way, I guess that's true. Devin told me when he saw me, he wanted to talk to me. I could have put a hold on that. Could have brushed it aside as something to do some other time.

But no...I had to go up on the stage while he was breaking down and tell him he did good tonight. He was better than good, though. The way he lit up the room on that stage was unreal. He had everyone hooked on every lyric. Even strum of his finger against the string. They got to feel the same emotion I did for so many nights.

That's why I approached him. His music has always had a way of pulling me toward him. A way of making me lose all reason and want to be in his presence. When he makes it big, I'm not sure where that will leave me. An ex-girlfriend thinking about all the good times? I hope not.

"Hey, Lisa." Eric calls from the bar as people file out of the building. "Are you okay?"

I don't miss the way his eyes cut to the stage where Devin is putting away his guitar. "Yeah. I'm good."

He nods and goes back to wiping down the bar as the other bartender's finish closing out tabs. I think the conversation is over, but after a few moments, he asks a question. "When do you want to start moving in?"

Devin just happens to be walking in front of the bar, and I see him flinch at the question. Ugh. I can already tell I'll have to set boundaries with Eric. I appreciate the big brother act, but it's not something I need. "We'll talk about that later."

Devin passes the stand and I smile at him. "I'll see you in a bit. It shouldn't take us long to clean up."

He looks back at the bar and nods. "I'll get the truck warmed up."

As soon as Devin is out the door, I march toward the bar. "I know we work together, and we'll be rooming soon, but I don't need you to step in." He opens his mouth to speak but I hold up a finger. "I appreciate the help, but hold off on giving it until I ask for it."

"Understood." Eric puts his hands up in surrender. At least he has the sense not to argue with me.

I turn away from the bar and stop in my tracks to face him again. "We're going to have to put together a list of boundaries when we become roomies, aren't we?"

Carlos passes by and laughs. "You can try, but I doubt it will do any good with that one. He's nosy by nature."

"You should give me some credit," Eric scoffs. "I'm not that bad." He wipes the same spot on the bar again. "Y'all just have a problem with seeing what's right in front of your face. I happen to be the one who points it out."

They are both too nosy for their own good. I have a feeling I'll have to set boundaries with both of them butting into my business. "I'm perfectly capable of seeing things. I don't need help in that area."

With that last warning, I head to the dining area and help the waitstaff wipe down the tables. I missed this monotonous work. It's the same type of work I picked up while traveling, but doing it in this bar feels different.

Carlos's song playlist is playing through the sound system to make the work go by faster. Even though it's work...it feels like I'm with my family. Something I only feel here and have never felt with the people I share a blood relationship with. How is that even possible? I'm lucky to have found these amazing people and the fact they took me in when they didn't have to.

The tables and floors are clean. The only thing left to do is clock out and get my stuff. It's been a long and exhausting first day back. Now, on top of that, I have to talk to Devin.

I'm not sure what possessed me to approach him. My normal response is to run from things that scare me. Not anymore. If I want to make Asheville my home, I need to learn to coexist with Devin. Chances of avoiding him are slim since he's my best friend's brother, and also performing here. I mean, I could always ask for different shifts, but I'd be leaving money on the table. Weekends are the best time for tips and a lot of traffic in the bar. I won't allow my past with him to derail my future happiness.

Sliding my arms into my jacket, I head toward the door. "See y'all tomorrow."

"Sure thing," Carlos waves. "Be careful tonight." He nods toward the door. He's not exactly subtle in giving the warning against Devin, but he means well.

"Okay." I push the door open, and the waiting area fills with cold air.

"Lisa," Eric calls. "Don't forget we need to figure out a day for you to move in."

"I know." Shaking my head, I step into the frigid wintry night. Yep, definitely going to have to make rules with him. Despite that, I think he'll be a good friend to have in my corner.

A black truck with a lift pulls up in front of me. I move toward it to get in, but Devin gets out and rushes to my side. He opens the door, and holds my hand as I climb in. That's something I haven't done in six months. It should feel weird to me. It doesn't though. Accepting his hand for help feels as natural now as it did then.

He closes the door behind me and gets in on the driver's side. "Do you want anything to eat?"

In all honesty, I'm starving. The only problem is, I don't want this late-night drive to feel like a date. "I'm fine."

My stomach growls, betraying me. "I'll run through a drive thru. Where do you want to go?"

"Whatever is closest is fine." He puts the truck in drive and pulls out of the lot. "But really, you don't have to stop. I can eat when I get home."

"Lisa, your body is clearly telling you it needs food. It's not that big of a deal." He drives another mile before pulling into the first burger place, he sees. Luckily, there isn't anyone in line. "Do you still like the same thing?"

Nodding I keep my focus anywhere but on him. I don't want him to see the shock on my face over him remembering what I like from this specific place.

He places my order and we pull around to the window. Very few cars are out at this time of night and I count them as they pass the restaurant. Anything to keep my mind busy and my focus off him. I'm not ready to talk about how we can be in the same circles without having anything going on between us. That conversation is meant for back roads and dashboard lights. Not this well-lit area under the awning.

He must sense my need for distraction because he doesn't say anything. I try to hand him my card to pay, but he waves it off. This definitely feels like it could fall into date territory so easily. After a few moments, the guy working the window hands him two bags and drinks. Devin passes them off to me so I can get them situated. It's a routine we've done many times before. The actions so familiar. I set the drinks in the cup holders in the console between us. He pulls away from the window as I search through the bags to see which one is mine.

"Do you want your food now, or do you want to wait?" His bag of food is in my lap, and I need to know if I should unwrap his burger.

"You can eat first." He turns on the radio and changes it to a station local to our county. Music much like what he plays comes through the speakers. "We can talk when you're done."

I don't wait for him to say anything else. Setting his bag aside, I grab mine and eat the fries first. People who can eat them cold are monsters, including Delilah. She actually prefers them cold. It may be the biggest thing we disagree about in our friendship. In the grand scheme of things that isn't too bad. Unless, of course, you count the fact that I dated her brother against her wishes and in secrecy. That might be a huge roadblock in our friendship.

Devin drives out of town and toward the area Stella lives in. It's still technically part of Asheville, but they kind of exist on their own out here. There aren't any stores nearby and most of the people who live out here don't have neighbors close to them. I'm all for adventure, but I like only having to drive five to ten minutes for anything I need.

He notices I'm almost done with my burger and as I chew, he asks, "What did you want to talk about?"

The time for communication has come. I swallow my food and take a drink. Prolonging the answer, a little longer. It's pitch black out here aside from the glow of the dashboard. It casts a soft blue light on his face, and I remember all the times we did this over the summer. His hands on this wheel as he told me his dreams. And me with my feet on the dash, the window down, letting in the night breeze and sounds of wildlife.

Now isn't the time to go down memory lane, though. We need to be on the same page if we're going to be around each other as much as I think we will be. There's no time like the present to find out the first bit of information. "How often do you play at the bar?"

"As much as they'll let me right now." I watch him as he runs a hand over his face. "If they bring in more acts sooner than later, it will be less. But Angie has me on the calendar for both nights every weekend."

That's going to be a problem. Well, not if we can agree to a friend's only relationship. I can't have anything else with him without hurting his sister, and that's something I refuse to do. "Okay." I take a deep breath and ask what I've been dreading since I came into town. "Did you tell Delilah about us?"

"God, no." He scoffs and turns down a road I haven't been on. If it were anyone else, I wouldn't be out here. But I trust him, even if we both hold some sort of hurt between us. "I'm still here, aren't I? Delilah is sweet and cuddly to most people, but if I had told her she would have lost her shit on me."

That's actually really good to know. "You know she can never find out, right?"

"What if we decide to give us another shot?"

This isn't exactly what I expected him to say. I guess I shouldn't be surprised, though. Not after the way he acted the other night when he overheard the roommate conversation. It was only a matter of time.

"Um, I don't think that's a good idea." Not only because it'll be against Delilah's wishes, which I have no intention of breaking again. But because it will never work out between us. When he catches the eye of a record label, and I have no doubt he will, where will that leave me? I've made the decision to stay in one place. I can't do that if he's traveling around the country. If I know him the way I think I do, he'll want me to go with him.

Devin pulls over on the side of the road. At first, I think it's because he wants to eat his food, but as soon as the truck is in park, he takes off his seat belt and turns toward me.

The heater blowing full blast is the only sound for a few seconds. He takes a sip of his soda and sets it down. "Why not? I like you and I think you still like me, too. I don't see a problem here."

I sit up straight and face him full on. "What do you mean you don't see a problem?" I throw my hands up in the air. "It's a huge problem. Delilah told us last time we were off limits to each other. We went behind her back and dated anyway. Do you honestly think this time will be any different?"

He shrugs and holds his hand out. I'm not sure what he wants so I place his food in his hand. He's not getting any sort of affection from me. Not after that doozy. "Yes, I do."

"How?" I shake my head and wipe my hand over my face. "If you can give me solid reasons why you think it would be different this time, I'll consider it." I won't, not really, but he doesn't know that. Anything to stop this conversation from going any further.

He laughs, like this is going to be easy. "I'll be able to see you more because you're working at the bar again. And I don't think Delilah will have an issue with it because she's in a relationship now, and happy. There's no reason for her to have anything against us dating. She won't want her best friend and brother to be unhappy."

He can't be serious. There's no way in actual hell he thinks that is the reason she didn't want us together. "You realize her being happy had nothing to do with it, right?"

"What other reason could it be?"

"You don't know your sister at all. It's because she didn't want to be overlooked by other people yet again. From what she's told me, she's always been someone in the background to your successes. This is about her boundaries and having something to herself. She wants to be someone's first choice." Did I say too much? Probably. But I don't really care. He needs to get it through his thick skull about how his sister feels.

"That's ridiculous," he grins. "She doesn't feel that way."

He is never going to get it. "You should probably talk to Delilah. She can shed some light on how she's feeling. Until then, we need to agree that we'll be nice to each other when we're in the same spaces. Especially while I'm living with Delilah. Work will be fine because you're on stage and I'm on the floor. Can we be cordial?"

"So, you're really moving in with Eric?" A flash hurt crosses his eyes. This isn't something I want to get into with him. Not right now, anyway.

"Yes." I nod to cement the point. "You won't be able to talk me out of it, either."

He runs a hand through his hair. "I just don't think it's a good idea. He has a reputation for hitting on lots of women. I don't want you to fall for his flirting."

"And what?" I throw my hands up. "I'm not capable of handling things myself? I've done pretty well for the past eight years."

The truck is silent aside from the heater, and I take a few calming breaths. I've never lost my temper with him. Not even close. But tonight...I couldn't contain it. I appreciate every-one's help, but when will they realize I'm strong enough to handle myself?

"I think you should take me back to my car." I turn toward the front of the truck to curb any desire he has to argue. And here I thought we were going to find a way to be friendly. I guess that was too much to hope for.

6
devin

WELL, that didn't go how I planned. I was trying to soften her up. Hoping like hell she would give us another chance. All I managed to do is piss her off. Then the stuff she said about my sister. That can't be true. Delilah would tell me if that's how she felt, wouldn't she?

Lisa is staring out the passenger window as I drive us back into town. The silence is heavy and I don't know how to fix it. This isn't something that's happened before. We've never had a problem talking. There was never a dull moment. It seems I've ruined that now.

"I'm sorry." It's the only thing I know to say to lessen the tension. And I really am sorry. My intention has never been to hurt her.

She continues staring out the window. "It's fine."

I can tell by her tone it's not. She doesn't want to get into another argument with me. "I'm serious, Lisa. I'll leave any sort of relationship talk about us alone. I won't even approach the subject until you're ready."

A spare a quick glance in her direction to see to her reaction. Her focus is on me now. "What if I'm never ready?"

I flinch at the question. That's definitely not what I want to hear, but all I can do is accept what she wants. For now, at least. "Then that will have to be okay." Doesn't mean I won't try to get her to fall head over heels for me again, but she doesn't need to know that.

"And what about our interaction in front of groups? We're going to have to get along if we're going to be around each other a lot." Her arms are crossed over her chest, and I can see her knee bobbing up and down. A sign that she's nervous. My answer has to be spot on.

"We're getting along now. I don't know why that will be any different around other people." Forget the way my eyes follow her around a room. If other people notice, that isn't my fault. I'll try though.

She takes a deep breath and lets it out. "Good." She nods and adjusts her jacket. "Then we should be good to go."

The lights along the street of Asheville are welcoming our arrival into town. The night is ending far sooner than I hoped but it's probably for the best. At least until we both get a hold of our emotions. Tomorrow night when I see her at the bar, things will be better. I plan on talking to my sister tomorrow. Not to seek her permission to date Lisa, but to feel around about what she would think about the possibility. Also, to see if she does feel like she comes second to me in everything. I've never wanted her to feel that way, and I need my sister to know that.

Moments after crossing the line into town, Lisa starts cleaning up her food mess. She has the bag in one hand and slides her purse into her lap with the other. I must have really pissed her off if she's going to bail as soon as I pull into the lot.

Out of the Ashes comes into view, and I slow down to enter the lot. Lisa's car is the only one on the side of the building. Carlos must have already gone home. Pulling to a stop next to it, Lisa reaches for the door handle.

"Hey, hold on." I grab her arm before she can get out. She faces me with an eyebrow raised. "Are we good?"

"Yes, Devin. We're fine." She pulls the handle and pushes the door open. "I guess I'll see you when you come play tomorrow night."

"Yeah." She has her hand on the edge of the truck door, pausing before she pushes it close. "I know I don't have the right to ask, but can you text me when you get home? Just to make sure you made it okay."

"Yeah." She holds the food trash up. "Thank you for the food."

"You're welcome," I nod at her, and the door closes with a thud. I really wish this wasn't the end of the night. Or, that things weren't so tense between us. I guess that's my fault, though. Dad's right about one thing...I tend to stick my foot in my mouth more often than not.

I'm not sure what that says about me. I don't remember that being an issue the last time we dated, but it only happens around Lisa. She's my weak spot and no matter what I do, I can't get her out of my head.

After a few minutes, Lisa is pulling out of the parking lot. I may not be able to handle things very well with her, but I can make sure she is on her way. Now that she's gone, I can head home. If I'm lucky tonight will give me some inspiration on music to write. The band is going to want new stuff to play if we'll be performing at the bar regularly.

* * *

My bandmates are warming up in the garage when I walk in. We really need to come up with a name for us. Right now, we're announced as my name. It's not fair to the rest of the guys. While I'd like to be a solo act, I'll have a band backing me up as well. If I can progress with my original guys, even better.

"I heard you killed it last night on your own," Cash calls out over the drums. How the hell did he know that?

"Yeah, it wasn't too bad." I rub the back of my neck. "Nothing like how we are on stage together."

"Don't forget about us when you're famous," he smirks. He always acts like I'd leave them behind. That's not happening.

"And what is up with hanging out with one of them employees late last night?" Trey strums on the guitar strings and grins. "My sister said you had a pretty blonde in the truck with you when you went through the drive thru."

"That was Lisa. She is one of the hosts at the bar." What is with them being all in my business? They aren't usually ones for town gossip. "And we're friends. So, whatever you think you have to say...don't."

"It was just a question." Trey holds his hands up. "We were just wondering if you finally found a girlfriend so you'll stop writing sad, sappy shit. It'll be nice playing something upbeat."

"We have upbeat songs." I don't know why I'm arguing with this man. "Even if we were dating, I'd probably write more love songs. So, I don't know how that would fix the problem."

"He likes her," Cash points a drum stick at me. "Who is this girl? I've only recently seen her at the bar."

"She worked there last summer before leaving for a trip. Now she's back." Maybe giving them some information will keep them from asking more questions. Or even insinuating there's something more than there is, no matter how much I wish that were true.

"I see," Trey wiggles his eyebrows up and down. "I think someone has a crush."

"Don't start, Trey." I roll my eyes. "She's my sister's best friend. That's the only reason I know." A small lie never hurt anyone. The less they know, the less can get back to my sister. Lisa wasn't wrong about that. She's never been great about sharing.

"Who is my best friend?" Delilah calls from the open garage door. It's like talking about her summoned her.

Trey opens his mouth, but I speak before he has a chance. My sister doesn't need to know Lisa and I went for a drive last night. "Lisa."

"Oh, yeah," she smiles. "She's actually the reason I'm here."

Shit. Did she say something to her? This can't be good if she did. She doesn't look mad. At least, I don't think she does.

"What about her?" I think my voice went up an octave at the end of the question. I hurry over to the fridge along the back wall and grab a water. My desperate attempt to act like I'm only thirsty.

She steps further into the garage. "I want to throw her a welcome home party since she's back for good. But I need some help?"

"Your friends at the bar can't help?" There's no way she actually thinks I'd have anything to offer. The one time my parents roped me into helping plan something special for Delilah's birthday, I totally screwed it up. Normally, they combine our parties because we're twins, but that particular year, they wanted to split them up. I get it. My friends didn't exactly mesh with her and her friends. It was better all the way around, but I slipped about the party and my mom got mad.

"It's an all hands on deck situation," she points toward the fridge, "can you toss me a water?"

I do as she asks and grab her a water. Her personality now is completely different than when we were teens. Hell, even from a few months ago. Love looks good on her, and it's someone who was a part of my inner circle which makes it even better.

"Between work, practice, and playing at the bar, I don't know when I'll have time."

"Please, Dev." She sets the water down and holds her hands together. "It would mean a lot to me, and I'm sure it'd mean a lot to her."

Both of my band mates look at me and I shrug my shoulders. There's no way she can know I was seeing Lisa last summer. We were careful. "If I have time, I'll help." That should appease her for now.

"Thanks, bro," she throws her arms around my neck and hugs me, "you are the best."

"If you say so." She won't think that if she finds out about my past with her. I wanted to talk to her about it, but not now. She's happy, and I refuse to do anything to make my sister sad. Not after my last screw up. Maybe Lisa is right. I need to have a heart to heart with my sister. But not now. Not here with the audience we have.

"You're playing tonight, right?" She eyes the three of us.

"Hell, yeah we are," Trey pumps his fist in the air. "We are going to rock that stage."

Delilah laughs and shakes her head. "Calm down. I know y'all will do great. Especially if you play the way you did on New Year's Eve."

"We can do that." Cash hits the cymbal with the drum stick.

Ugh. She's getting them all riled up. Now they'll be insufferable while we practice for tonight's set. She turns toward the door, and I call out her name.

"Del, are you working tonight?"

"Yep. I'll be there."

"Awesome," I sigh in relief. "Can you make sure the door to the alley is unlocked? I don't think it'll be a good look if we're carrying our equipment through the front door. And it'll be hard to maneuver between tables and people."

"Yeah. If for some reason it's still locked, call me and I'll let you in." She waves at me, "Carlos doesn't like to leave it unlocked in case whoever is closing forgets to lock it back."

"Understandable." I wave back. "I'll see you tonight."

With that, my sister leaves and we can finally begin practice. We only have a few hours before we have to load up my truck and get ready. Not that we do a full wardrobe change. It's just a new pair of jeans, slightly nice shirts, and a ball cap for me.

"Devin," Cash calls out to me. "Get your head out of the clouds. We have to warm up. You aren't going to impress Lisa if we sound like shit."

"Who said I'm trying to impress her?" It's a little ridiculous that is the first conclusion they jump to.

"Please," Cash rolls his eyes. "You have that love sick expression on your face. It's been there since we brought her up. What's holding you back?"

"Aside from the fact she's Del's best friend? She wants nothing to do with me." At least not romantically. She made it very clear last night she wants us to be on friendly terms at best. Even that felt forced. I honestly think she doesn't want any interaction with me.

"Why don't you let us be the judge of that?" Trey adjusts his guitar strap and points to the mic. "For now, let's practice. I have a new idea for one of our regular songs."

This is why I could never leave these two behind. They constantly want to improve our songs, and I'm excited for the twist Trey wants to do. As for them being witness to whatever form of rejection Lisa wants to throw my way, they'll see I'm right. If I'm wrong, I'm okay with that point being proven as well.

Sitting here stressing over something I have no control over isn't going to help us get these songs ready before tonight. "Alright, let's do this."

Cash counts off the time with his drum sticks and music fills the garage. At least this is something I love and can control.

7

lisa

"YOU ARE BEING SECRETIVE." Delilah is pushing something off the table, and into her pocket, as I walk into the dining area. She's on break, and I'm about to watch what happens behind the bar. Carlos wants me to see what it's like on a busy night before I make a firm decision on getting my bartending license.

"I don't know what you're talking about." Delilah grins up at me. "I was just making a list of things I need to do around the house."

"Then you won't have a problem showing me." I have a feeling she's planning something for me. She's as bad as her brother at keeping secrets so I don't know why she won't tell me whatever she's doing.

"Really, it's not that big of a deal." She pats her pocket to make sure the paper is all the way inside. "Just some renovations that need to be done. Bryce pointed out a few things before Christmas and I want to get started on them."

That's believable but I don't think that's what she was writing down. But now is a good time to bring up my plans to move out. "About that."

"About what?" She looks over at me. "The renovations?"

"No," I shake my head. "I'm actually moving out."

"What!" She stands and knocks the chair back a few inches. "What do you mean you're moving out? You just got here. You can't be leaving again."

Placing my hands on her shoulders, I meet her eyes. "I'm not leaving Asheville, so calm down."

"Then why are you moving out?"

I glance toward the door to make sure nobody is coming in. "Because you and Bryce have your own thing going on, and me staying with you was only temporary."

"But...I like having you there. I can tell Bryce not to come over as much." Her shoulder sag like I've taken away her favorite toy.

"Don't be silly." I let go of her, but don't move away. "You two need to live your life without me interfering. What happens when he inevitably moves in? I love you and love that you're happy, but I don't want to be the third wheel. Besides, it's not like I'm going far."

"Fine," she rolls her eyes. "I guess I see your point. Where are you moving?"

At least she doesn't seem as upset anymore. Honestly a small part of her seems to be relieved. As much as she wants me there, I know she's enjoyed having Bryce there all the time. I was right about putting a cramp in her style. "Eric has an extra bedroom in the house he rents from Carlos. So, I'm moving in over there."

"Oh, dear God." She shakes her head and runs her hand down her face. "Please do not let him flirt his way into your bed."

"Gross," I swat at her arm. "That is not happening. He's cute and all, but I'm not one to easily for corny pickup lines."

"At least you know what he's capable of."

"You're not mad, right?"

Delilah wraps her arms around me in a giant hug. "Of course not, silly. You have to do what makes you happy. I can support that." Her finger is in my face as soon as the words leave her mouth. "But do not bail on Asheville again. I will hunt you down."

"Yes, ma'am." I salute her. The bell above the door jingles. "I should probably tend to whoever is coming in."

She waves me away, "Don't worry about it. I've got it, you go do whatever you need to. I've got it."

We leave the dining area and I glance over my shoulder. A whole group of people come in and I feel bad she has to deal with them. I do need to get behind the bar, though. Tonight, will help me determine if this is something I want to do.

Eric and Carlos are already pouring drinks. The customers are coming in quick now that the sun has gone done and there's a promise of live music. "Hey, Lisa," Eric smiles up at me. "Ready to see us in action?"

"Sure." It's a good thing I'm a people person. They are talking to everyone as they make their drinks. Well, Eric is. Carlos just makes the drinks with minimal conversation. He still makes pretty good tips based on the jar on his side of the bar.

Out of the corner of my eye, I see Delilah mess with her phone before setting it under the bar. "I'm going to see if she Del needs any help. Be right back."

I rush from behind the bar and am beside Delilah in seconds. "You good? You look flustered."

'Actually, can you go unlock the door to the alley? My brother and his band just pulled up and need to bring their instruments in."

"Um, yeah, sure." I glance at the gathering crowd in front of the door. I almost offer to take over host duties, but that would take more time than it would to unlock the door.

Besides, it's not like I have to talk to Devin or anything. I have one job. Unlock the door. Easy peasy.

I weave in and out of the crowd until I'm on the side of the stage. There's a small hallway behind it where the door to the alley is located. Someone is knocking on the door as I approach it. Dang. It's like they can't give one of us time to get back here. I mean, it's not like we all have other things we have to do. Aside from me tonight, I guess. My sole job tonight is to watch Carlos and Eric behind the bar.

With my hand on the handle, I push the door open. Except it doesn't. At least, not all the way. I hear an "oof" on the other side. One of these geniuses is standing directly in front of the door.

Someone else laughs, "Shit, man, your nose is bleeding."

I stick my head out to see what happened. I don't know who the guys standing to the left are, but the person with the bloody nose is none other than Devin. Shit. Of course, it would be him. "Can one of you pull him out of the way?"

The guy with a guitar case grabs his arm and pulls him from in front of the door. Pushing the door all the way open, I try to assess the damage. The lighting isn't the best and I can see blood on the hand Devin is using to try to stop the bleeding. Ugh, Carlos is going to kill me for injuring one of the musicians despite how he feels about him.

"I know you aren't my biggest fan, but you didn't have to hit me with the door." Devin's voice is muffled. It's a wonder I could make any of it out.

"Let me see your case." I hold my hand out waiting for him to give it to me. I motion to the guys, "Follow me." Devin is close behind me. He probably can't see since his head is tilted back. I reach backward and grab his arm. After I set his guitar on the floor behind the stage, I turn toward his band mates. "You can go ahead and set up. There's a first aid kit in the office. We're going to see if we can stop the bleeding. Come on Devin."

My hand slides down his arm until I'm grasping his. Despite how cold it is outside, his hand is warm. I feel the calluses he's built-up playing guitar against my skin. If I said I didn't miss this one small act of intimacy, it would be a lie. Holding his hand feels natural, and the gentle squeeze he gives me tells me he's feeling the same way. Shit. This is not good.

I pick up the pace, and he manages to keep up despite dealing with a nose bleed. Hopefully that's all it is, and I didn't unintentionally break his nose.

There is a small gap between customers and we catch Eric's attention. His eyes widen and he moves toward the opening of the bar. But at the slight shake of my head, he stops in his tracks. I'm sure he'll have a million questions when I get back there, and I'll do my best to answer them. He's like a dog with a bone...he'll never let it rest until I give him all the details. It's funny what you learn about people in such a short amount of time.

We turn into the hallway that leads to the office, and I can finally slow our pace. There aren't any lines for the bathroom and very few lingering eyes. The likelihood of gossip happening over this minimal. Thank God. The last thing I need is someone misconstruing the situation and it getting back to Delilah.

I throw the office door open, pulling Devin inside, and shut it behind us. Releasing his hand, I turn toward him. "I'm so, so sorry."

Despite his hand covering the lower part of his face, his eyes are lit with amusement. Seriously, I hit him with a door and he's smiling about it?

"You can slam a door into my face as many times as you want if it means I get to hold your hand."

"You're ridiculous." I throw my hands up, and move

around him. Scanning the shelves, I look for the first aid kit. It's here somewhere. Angie is so clumsy, we keep extras on hand, but I don't see it anywhere. Clearly, it's not on this wall, I move to the other wall and feel Devin's eyes on me. "I mean, who the hell stands directly in front of a door when they know someone is coming to open it?"

It's not on these shelves either. I stop for a moment running through all the places it could be. My eyes bounce around the room before landing on the desk. That has to be where it's at, and I rush over there. I'm not sure what time he has to be on stage, but I know every minute in here is a delay. It's also a chance for me to fall for his charm, and I can't. Especially not after last night.

"In my defense," he pauses and I glance in his direction. He's grabbing one of the rags off the shelf closest to him and shoves it over his nose. "The door was supposed to be unlocked. I'm guessing my sister forgot to remind management."

"Having bands here is still new. I'm sure it won't be a problem once we get into a routine." I pull open the top drawer of the desk. It's not here. The next drawer provides nothing. There's only one more drawer I can get into. The last one is locked, and I'll have to ask Carlos for the key. Which means I'll have to explain what happened.

Please for the love of all things holy be in this drawer. I slide the drawer open and a big white box labeled First Aid sits atop a stack of papers. I begin pulling it out of the drawer when his words stop me. "It was still worth it."

Glancing up I expect him to be where he was, but he's right in front of the desk. "That is the dumbest thing I've ever heard. You better hope it's not broken and I just busted it up."

He shrugs. "Girls dig scars."

"Not when they know how you got them," I mutter under my breath. I set the kit on top of the desk and rummage through. There are cleaning wipes and a few small bandages. Pulling them out, I set them on the desk and point to one of the chairs in front of it. "Sit down so I can see the damage."

He does as he's told and waits for me to pull up a chair in front him. "I don't remember you being so bossy before you left. I think I like it."

"And I don't remember you being so maddening." I set the supplies in my lap and lean toward him. As gently as I can, I pull the rag away from his face. Plus side...it wasn't gushing blood. He does have it streaked from his upper lip to his chin. I dap the rag over his nose trying to get off as much blood as possible. This would be much easier if the rag was wet.

"So, how does it look?" Devin asks. His gaze focused on me. "Will I need to go to the doctor?"

It's the first time I've heard a hint of concern from him. Maybe all the flirting was a distraction so I wouldn't know how much pain he's in.

"I'm not sure." I open up the wet wipes. "I can't get a good look at it. Is it okay if I—" Holding up the wipe, I silently ask his permission.

He nods in answer. I take a corner of the towelette and wipe the top of his nose. He winces, and I immediately pull my hand away. Awful doesn't begin to describe what I'm feeling right now. "It's okay, Lisa." He grabs my hand and lifts it up. "I'll be fine."

This is completely outside of my set of skills. How am I supposed to know if it's broken or not? "Okay." I brush the wipe against his nose and his jaw clenches. So much for being fine. But if I stop now, I won't be able to finish. After a few moments I've got most of the blood cleared away.

"What's the verdict?"

"There's a cut, and it's definitely swollen, but I can't tell if it's broken." Maybe I should take some sort of first aid training. Or, I can get Del to call her boyfriend. He knows what to do in these instances.

"Damn," he breathes. "Do you have anything I can take for the pain?"

"Yeah, there's some ibuprofen in here. Why?"

"I need to get out there. I'm sure Cash and Trey are wondering where I'm at." He stands and holds a hand out to help me up.

"Okay." I let him pull me out of the chair. "Let me grab the medicine from the kit." Moving back behind the desk, I rummage around for what he asked. I grab the packet and look up to hand it to him. "Um, you might have a bigger problem."

"Like what? I already have a busted nose and need to clean my face."

I point to the red splotches on his shirt. "You have some blood on your clothes." Now I feel even worse. Not only did I hit him in the face, but I've ruined his clothes. I doubt he'll ever be able to get that out.

"Shit," he shakes his head. "At least it's mostly dark over there. It shouldn't be too noticeable."

"Hold on," I hand him the packet and a warm bottle of water I pull out of the package by the desk. "I think we have some employee shirts here somewhere. What's your size?"

The shelf to my right is where the aprons are stored. I rummage through the various pieces of cloth until I find the stack of shirts. There aren't many options, but we'll have to make do.

"I wear a medium. But honestly, it's not that big of a deal." He glances at his shirt. "Nobody will be close enough to notice."

Ignoring his protests, I flip through until I find a black shirt. They have the bar logo on it, but it'll be fine. Turning around I start to toss the shirt to him, but he's right in front of me and my hand meets his chest. "You really shouldn't sneak up on people like that."

"And you should listen. It'll be fine." When he feels me push the shirt to him with force, he relents. "But I'll wear this."

He doesn't grab it just yet. Instead...he pulls the shirt he's wearing over his head, tossing it behind him. It's like he's trying to get under my skin. And he knows this is the best way to do it because it's distracting as fuck. "Wh-what are you doing?"

"You told me to change so that's what I'm doing," he smirks. With blood on his face, and a busted nose, he shouldn't look so hot. Shouldn't be as enthralling as he is. "Unless that's not what you want me to do."

He moves toward me until my back hits the shelf. I could side step him, but I don't know if I want to. "What are you doing?"

He bends down until his eyes meet mine. As if my focus is on anything but him. "Trying to make you realize you still have feelings for me. That there's still a connection between us."

Damn him. He's making this harder than it needs to be. The attraction and feelings toward him have never changed. It's why I left Asheville to begin with. "That was never the issue, and you know it."

"I know," he leans closer to me. His lips are inches away from mine and I can feel myself leaning toward him. Closing the distance and feeling wanted like I've seldom felt in my entire life. He shifts until his mouth brushes my ear. "But we can change that this time around. We can do it right."

It takes everything in me to keep from leaning into him. To saying fuck it and realize I deserve happiness despite how it will make others feel. In the end, I can't fight it. Can't fight the pull he has on my heart. I turn and our lips brush.

He pulls me toward him and deepens the kiss. His fingers curling into my hair to keep me close. I've missed this so much, and it feels like coming home. The way his mouth moves over mine, claiming me and letting me know I'm his. As much as we shouldn't be doing this, it's good to know he still has this reaction to me.

The door opens. "Hey Lisa, Carlos wants to know…" The words die on Eric's lips.

I jump away from Devin, reality slamming down on me. "This," I wave my hands between us, "can't happen again."

Mortification reddens my cheeks. Dropping the shirt on the floor, I rush toward the door. Before I walk out, I stop beside Eric. "Not a word to anyone."

I hope like hell he can keep his mouth shut. What happened back there is why I can't be left alone with Devin. All my old feelings come rushing back, and I make choices that could ruin my friendship with Delilah. I can't chance that happening again.

8
devin

JUST FUCKING GREAT. I was finally getting through to her. Well, my lips were anyway, and we were interrupted. There's no way in hell she's going to give me the time of day now. She's scared and when that happens, she shuts down. I'll be lucky if she doesn't skip town again despite what she's told my sister.

I grab the shirt off the floor and pull it over my head, wincing when the fabric brushes against my nose. That kiss also took my mind off the fact she hit me in the face with a door. The pain is still worth the progress I made even though that's a moot point now.

With the shirt in place, I turn for the door, but it's blocked by Eric. He's glaring at me, and I'm itching for him to say something. He needs to know whatever crush he has on Lisa will never amount to anything else.

He takes a step forward and points in my direction. "I don't know what happened between the two of you in the past, but it needs to stop."

It's a good thing Lisa isn't here. She would be fuming. "Exactly, you don't know. But what I do know is she wouldn't want you sticking up for her. She's perfectly capable of handling her own battles."

The people who think they know a person never really do. Eric doesn't even fit the bill for knowing her. He wasn't here the last time she worked here. He didn't start working here until a month after she left. When she destroyed my heart by not even allowing me the chance to defend my reasons.

"I can tell," Eric says breaking me from my thoughts. He shakes his head, "Except you seem to be her blind spot. Every time I see the two of you together her body language shifts."

"You know she's never going to date you, right?" Is it shitty thing for me to say? Probably. But I need to get his anger off of me, and find out what his motivations are about Lisa.

"Of course, that's what you'd come back with." He turns back toward the door. "I know she won't date me. She's made that perfectly clear, and honestly, I was flirting with her that night because that's what I do with everyone. But everyone who works at this bar is like family to me, despite when they work here. I always protect my family."

With that threat looming in the air, he walks out. This wasn't supposed to be turned into a pissing contest, even though that's my fault. I also admire that he's protective over everyone here because that includes my sister. It's good to know she's got someone watching her back. The sad thing is, in this instance it's also from me.

Fuck. I really screwed things up today. Too bad I can't focus on that right now. I have a show to play. I grab the rag I was using earlier to staunch the bleeding and head to the bathroom. Getting cleaned up is the first priority. Then I need to join my band mates on the stage. They are probably wondering where I am.

The crowd from the bar is getting louder, and I know the people in front of the stage are getting restless. They came for a show and they'll get one.

A quick glance in the mirror and I'm taken aback. She wasn't lying when's she said there was blood everywhere. It's streaked down my chin. I run the rag under water, pump some soap into it, and start scrubbing. I don't have long, but I can't go out there like this.

* * *

We closed down the bar. Mostly because I was late coming on stage, but also because we were having a great time. I love playing with Cash and Trey. They take away any nerves I feel when I'm on stage, and they know how to hype a crowd better than I ever could. I have charisma, but nothing compared to them.

"Dude, we killed it out there. Even with your busted up nose changing your voice." Trey is loading up his guitar in the case. His ball cap is gone because he threw it in the crowd. It's weird seeing him without it. I actually don't think I ever have.

"Hell yeah," Cash adds. "Are we playing every weekend?"

"Yeah," I nod while putting the equipment away. "As long as that's okay with you. Angie said we can do both nights or just one night. Also, leave my nose out of the equation, Trey. It's not my fault I got hit in the face. It's a good thing I had y'all with me to mask my voice because if I was solo tonight, I'm not sure it would have gone as well."

"That's so awesome." Trey closes his case and starts wrapping cords. "I'm down for every weekend."

"Well, it's not forever. Just until they get some other acts booked." They may know some more people. "Speaking of, have y'all seen any acts looking for a place to play? The way I see it, if we have more bands playing here then more people will come aside from people that live in the area."

"I can ask around," Cash says. "There's never a shortage of bands wanting to book gigs."

"Sounds good." The bar is most empty. All the patrons have gone home and it's just the employees cleaning up the place. I want to get out their way, but at the same time...I need another chance to talk to Lisa. Once again, I fucked up by cornering her like that. Well, verbally anyway. Even though it wasn't all my fault. She turned to kiss me. She could have moved and gotten away from me. That action told me everything I needed to know. I only need to find a way to make things right and have her by my side.

"Are we ready to load up and head out?" Cash has all his drum equipment together. Right now, I'm kind of wishing we brought separate cars, but I'm the only one with a truck and it's easier to load everything into it than shoving it in back seats.

"Yeah, give me a sec." I could approach Lisa right now to see if she'll talk to me. I won't though. From what my sister has said Lisa hasn't changed her number so I shoot her a text instead.

DEVIN

Can we talk?

My eyes are focused on her to see if she'll check her phone. It never leaves her side, even when she's working. She doesn't disappoint. She pulls her phone out of her back pocket, reads the screen and her eyes meet mine from across the bar.

LISA

That's probably not a good idea.

DEVIN

Please. We don't have to do it here. Maybe you can come by after you get off.

LISA

Sorry. I rode over with Delilah.

DEVIN

> Breakfast tomorrow? We can even go over to the next town so nobody will see us together.

She looks at the phone, then at me. Indecision over what to do. Finally, her fingers move over the screen.

LISA

> Fine. But we can't make this a habit.

DEVIN

> I'll text you a time and place when I get home.

There's no response after that. I'm considering it a victory. Turning toward the guys, I wave to the instruments. "Let's hit the road."

* * *

My palms are clammy. I haven't had that issue since I was a teenager taking my first girlfriend out on a date. For whatever reason, Lisa evokes the same anxiety. I'm so terrified I'm going to screw things up. Say something I shouldn't because I can't seem to say the right thing to her.

My phone is sitting on the table and I tap the screen to check the time. She's late. People are coming in and out of the restaurant, going about their day. The waitstaff keeps glancing in my direction to see if the person I'm waiting for is going to show up. It's odd being on this side of pitying looks. It's not something I've ever experienced, and I know for a fact I don't like it. I refuse to order my meal until she gets here, and feel bed I'm taking up space when it's such a busy morning for the restaurant.

A part of me wants to grab my phone and walk out the door. If I do that, I'll feel like an asshole if she shows up. I don't want to be that guy. Especially not when it's one of her biggest fears. People walking out and abandoning her when she counted on them for everything. I won't be that person to her. I wasn't in the first place; we just couldn't agree on some things and she ran.

"Can I get you anything?" A girl about my age approaches the table.

This is the third time they've sent someone over, and even though I don't want to start eating without Lisa, I need to order something. "Coffee would be great. I haven't decided what I want to eat yet. Can you give me a few more moments?"

"Sure thing." Her voice is chipper, but the look in her eyes tells me everything I need to know. I've been stood up. She leaves to get my coffee, and I pick up the menu to look things over. No more waiting. Lisa has given me her answer despite how much I don't like it.

I'm so focused on finding the right breakfast item to match my heartbreak, I don't notice someone has slid into the booth in front of me. At least, not until she speaks. "Sorry, I'm late." Lisa sets her bag down beside her. "I debated whether or not I should come."

Setting the menu down, I study Lisa. She's not kidding. Her hair is thrown into a bun and she's wearing leggings and a sleep shirt. She must have decided when she was supposed to be here already. "I'm glad you came."

"You may not be by the time we leave." She grabs the menu in front of, lifting it in front her face so I can't see what she's thinking. "Have you ordered, yet?"

"No," I shake my head even though she can't see me. "I was waiting on you."

"Oh," she sets the menu down. "I'm really sorry. You should have ordered."

"It would have been awkward." That's the most honest

answer I have for her. I would have been sitting here, watching her eat, with nothing to fill the space.

"I can understand that."

"What made you decide to meet me?" The fact she is late hangs out there in the open.

She looks down at the menu this time, gathering her thoughts. "Closure? The kiss? Both? It's really hard to pinpoint exactly why I'm here. My feelings for you have never changed. But I can't be with you on the sly. I won't be treated like a dirty secret."

"I've never treated you that way."

"No, but you didn't want to tell the one person we should have. And that is what makes it feel gross. Delilah has a right to know, especially when she implied that we couldn't date each other."

"You realize we are grown, right? She can't exactly tell us who we are allowed to date."

"Yes, I know." She huffs in frustration. "It's a respect thing. I don't have siblings. Hell, I barely have a family. Excuse me for not wanting to fuck up the one good relationship I've had in my life."

Her voice has risen, and it's getting the attention of the other patrons. I place a hand on hers. "It's okay. We don't have to get into that right now."

The waitress comes back with my coffee and we place our breakfast order. It's the perfect distraction to break the tension coming from Lisa.

Once the waitress is gone, Lisa focuses on me once again. "We kind of do. That's the whole reason I left all those months ago. You wouldn't listen to me then, but I need you to now."

"Okay."

Taking a deep breath, she speaks. "Delilah is probably the best person I know. She took me in when I first came to town. Her opinion of me means more than anything. Then I met you and got swept up in a relationship. And it felt shitty keeping that from the most important person in my life. And when you doubled down on not telling her, that made things even worse. I couldn't in good conscience stay here, so I left. It was easier than telling her about us."

"I'm sorry about that." Running a hand through my hair, I exhale. "I was scared. Not only of how my sister would react, but also because I didn't know how things with us were going to pan out. I lo- liked you a lot." She doesn't need to know I'm in love with her. Not if we can't figure out a way to make this work. "I still do, but I haven't had the best track record with girlfriends. The last thing I wanted was to have Delilah feel like she'd be in the middle."

"Have you talked to her?"

Woah, that question is out of left field. "No. Cash and Trey were at the house when she came by, and I didn't feel having an audience around would be good."

The waitress shows up with our food and we dig in. I'm starving but the break in conversation is nice. I'm not sure where to go from here. Lisa must feel the same way because she hasn't said anything else. It's weird eating without any small talk. To be sitting here with so much I want to say and being left alone with my thoughts.

Once we're finished eating, Lisa digs through her bag for something. She pulls her wallet out and I wave it away. "Breakfast is on me."

"Are you sure?"

"Yeah."

She puts it back in her bag and leans back against the seat. "I know it's hard with me being back, but please talk to your sister. Maybe that will shed some light on why I'm so adamant on her knowing about us."

"After I talk to her, will you at least consider giving us another shot?"

"Yes," she closes her bag and stands up. "But you have to find out her general feelings about us dating. I can't go behind her back again."

"I will." I stand. "Can I at least give you a hug?"

She nods and I wrap my arms around her, squeezing her tight. Who knows, it might be the last time we hug each other. Releasing her, I watch her walk out of the restaurant. Once she's in her car, I call my sister.

9
lisa

THAT WAS A BAD IDEA. I shouldn't have gone. At least he knows how I feel and my reasoning. Guilt also flows through me because I was so late. I figured he would have gotten tired of waiting and left before I showed up. Then I wouldn't be feeling mixed up about my emotions.

On one hand, I'd give anything to date Devin again. He made me feel important and loved. Two things I never felt before coming to Asheville. Before, finding what it means to have family that will go to bat for you. On the other hand, I don't want to disrespect Delilah. Not after all she's done for me.

My whole body is shaking. I'm not sure if it's because I'm nervous about being around my best friend after this morning and the kiss I shared with her brother last night. Or, if it's because the heat in my car still hasn't warmed it up. It's probably a mixture of both. I didn't even tell her where I was going this morning. She was still asleep and I didn't want to bother her. She also would have asked what I was doing. That wasn't something I wanted to get into. Not until I had a chance to talk to Devin.

Finally, my heater decides to work at full capacity ten minutes from Asheville. A part of me doesn't want to go home yet. The need to put off any questions Delilah is going to throw at me. Should I have made Devin the sole person who needs to talk to her? Probably not. But I can't be the first person who talks to her about it. Not while I'm still living there.

Pulling into the driveway, I notice her car is gone. Bryce's car is there, though. That's weird. Unless of course they took her car. I don't know Bryce well. I saw him come in the bar a few times with his sister, but never talked to him. Even when he's been here with Delilah, I don't talk much. They have their own inside jokes and I feel like an outsider because I've been away for so long. I wasn't here when their relationship sparked.

The door is unlocked when I turn the knob and that can only mean one thing. Someone is home. Opening the door, I walk in to Bryce on the couch watching a movie. "Hey," I wave awkwardly. "Where's Delilah?"

He jumps up and pauses the movie. "Oh, hi." Setting the remote on the table he comes over to me. "Her brother called and said he needed her help with something."

"Just her?"

"Yeah. She's been gone about ten minutes. I'm not sure when she'll be back, but she has her phone on her if you need her for something."

"No, I was curious, that's all." Shit. He's doing it now? I thought he'd wait a day. Or a week, for that matter. He wasn't playing when he said he wanted another chance. I guess I should be happy he isn't putting it off, but a little warning would have been nice. Now I'm worried for when she comes home.

"I can, uh, head home if you want. We weren't sure when you'd be back."

"No," I wave him away. "You're fine. I'll probably see if Eric is awake so I can start moving stuff over there." Plus, it's the perfect way to avoid Delilah until I know what kind of mood, she's going to be in.

"Yeah, she mentioned you were moving out," he lifts a hand and rubs the back of his neck, "I hope it's not because of me. I never meant to make you uncomfortable if I did."

He really is a good guy, and I'm beyond happy my friend found someone that cares so much for not only her, but her friends. He's definitely a keeper.

"Not at all." Well, not entirely. "So much has happened since I was gone. I didn't want to be an intrusion on the two of you. I'm actually shocked you haven't moved in yet. You're here more than you're not."

"We've talked about it. But she didn't want to throw too many changes at you." That's a punch to the gut. Not because she's caring, but because she's putting off living her life to make sure I'm oaky. She really is the best, and I feel like shit because of the way I left with zero explanation. Who knows... after today she may not want to talk to me for a while.

"Y'all shouldn't base your decisions on me. Do what makes both of you happy." I mean that with every fiber of my soul. They both deserve happiness, and I won't be the one who stands in the way of that.

"Thanks." He grins and I wish I could have been here to see the two of them fall in love. "If you start moving today and need any help, just ask. It's not like I have anything better to do."

"I will." Pointing toward my room down the hallway, "I'm just gonna go."

"Okay. Please let me know if you need any help. Even if it's not at Eric's, I can help you load stuff in the car."

He really is very kind, and I feel bad for not trying to get to know him better. My steps are rushed as I make my way to my room. I need to shower, but I feel weird taking one with him here. I don't know why since I'll be in the same situation with Eric. But I've placed him firmly in the friend zone. There's no way anything is going to happen in regard to him. Even if Devin wasn't the one who has my heart.

I wasn't lying to Del last night when I told her corny pickup lines weren't my thing. If I had a nickel for every time some guy has tried the same shit as Eric when I worked at various bars, I'd be rich. Who told these guys that is the correct way to pick up ladies? It's something they need to change for sure.

Closing the door firmly behind me, I throw my keys on the dresser and my bag on the bed. I grab my phone from my leggings pocket and search through the contacts for Eric's number. Pressing his name, I wait for the phone to ring. I was going to text him, but I need the quick response from a phone call.

"Hello?" Great. He sounds like he was still asleep. Not that I blame him. It's rough getting enough sleep when you close the bar. I'm just happy we all get the day off. That's a new and welcome change Angie and Carlos have made. Back when I was here the first time, we worked seven days a week with a small staff. I guess that's the perk of having enough people to rotate.

"Hey, are you up?"

"I guess I am now. What's up?"

Studying my room, I try to figure out how much stuff I have. "Are you ready for me to be your roomie?"

"Sure. Though, it's kind of quick after our discussion the other night. Did something happen?" The concern in his voice is admirable.

"No." It's a lie. I'm running because I'm scared of the reaction Delilah will have after talking to Devin, but he doesn't need to know that. "I just figured since we're off today, it's probably best to do it now."

"Oh," he laughs, "that makes sense. Do you need me to come over and help pack your things?"

The way his tone switched when he realized I wasn't in trouble is amazing. He'll be a good friend to have at my side. In the short amount of time I've known him, I've come to realize he's the brother figure most girls have. He reminds me of a younger Carlos.

"No. I think I can get it all. Bryce said he can help me load everything into my car." All I need for now is the basics. I can come get my knick-knacks later. I glance at the bed and realize I forgot to ask before. "Does the room I'll be taking have a bed?"

"No. We'll need to get you one."

"Okay cool." I guess I'll need to buy an air mattress until then. Or, ask Delilah if she has one, I can borrow. We'll find out if she's in a giving mood later today. "I'll have my first load of things over there in about an hour. Is that cool?"

"Yep." I hear ruffling and I know he's getting out of bed. "See you then."

I hang up the phone and toss it on the bed. It's time to pack up my suitcase again. This time, though...I'm only going across town, not the other side of the state.

* * *

Eric takes his time to open the front door. It's cold and I'm only wearing leggings and a t-shirt. Bad planning on my part? Maybe, but that doesn't matter. I'm already stressed out over whatever Delilah and Devin are doing. Especially since I don't know how Del is reacting. Letting this interaction get under my skin is new for me, and I don't know what to do with those feelings.

The door swings open, and Eric is standing in front of me in sweatpants and a long-sleeved T-shirt. It's good to know he doesn't run around the house has naked because that would have to be a rule. It's not something I want to see from my roommates. Even Delilah comes out dressed, or in a long robe. It's common courtesy.

"Wow, you weren't lying about being over here an hour. It's an hour on the dot."

"I don't know if I should be offended or not for being punctual." He's still standing in front of the door and I cock my head to the side. "Are you going to let me in? Or is there some secret handshake we need to do before I'm allowed entrance?"

He laughs and moves to the side. "I mean there isn't one right now, but the fact that you brought it up makes me want to have a secret handshake."

I step inside the house with my suitcase behind me. "You do realize we aren't twelve, right?"

"Why are you trying to make me grow up faster than I'm ready?" He looks like I genuinely hurt his feelings. The sad puppy eyes, the pouty mouth, and everything. Living with him is going to be interesting, but at least it will never be dull.

"Sorry for raining on your parade."

"Do you have anything else in the car you need to grab?" He looks over my shoulder toward my car in the driveway.

Normally, I'm not the type of person to accept help but I think today is an exception. "Actually, there are a couple of boxes involved in my backseat, if you can grab those."

"No problem," he takes a step outside barefoot. This man is going to get sick. I wonder if his mom had to stay on him about dressing weather appropriate when he was a kid. Not like I'm one to talk right now, but this is about him, not me. "I don't remember if Carlos showed you the room, but if you go down the hall it's the last door on the left."

"Thanks." Pulling my suitcase behind me, I make my way down the hall until I'm standing in front of my new room. Moving in with people I don't know very well has never been a problem but this time it feels different. I'm not sure if it's because I have intentions of staying here in Asheville. Or, if it's because I'm living with a man when my eyes and heart are stuck on another. Especially, when I know Devin does not like the idea of me living with Eric.

There is nothing he can do about it though. Even if we were dating, I wouldn't move in with him right off the bat. We need that time to learn and grow and be able to be in a relationship out in the open. Until that happens, moving in with him would be the last thing on my list.

I open the door and step inside. The room is about the same size as the one I have at Delilah's. At least the space isn't smaller. I have room to spread out, and decorate to my heart's content. There are two dressers along the wall. It's weird that Carlos decided to leave those but took the bed. He must have needed it for his girlfriend's son or his sisters. That is the first thing I need to buy. Thank goodness I don't need anything fancy. I'm used to getting by with the bare minimum. It's a hazard of moving from place to place.

"Where do you want me to put these?" I jump at the sound of his voice and my suitcase falls to the floor.

"Jesus." I breathe out. "Are you always this quiet?"

"Do I need to stomp to make my presence known?" He's laughing. Yeah, life here will definitely be interesting.

"Or wear a damn bell." That is a more viable option. Maybe he needs to wear one at work, too. It would prevent any awkward situations like what happened last night. Though if he hadn't come through the door, I don't know if I would have stopped kissing Devin. My reservations be damned.

"Mmm," he grimaces. "I think that's where I'll draw the

line."

"Understandable. You can set the boxes anywhere." It's not like there isn't enough space in here. At least, until I get a bed. I think that's what is going to make this feel real. I don't even remember the last time I bought furniture. If it required having to move it, I did without. This is huge for me.

"Are you staying here tonight, or at Delilah's?" He places the boxes on the floor against the far wall. "It doesn't matter to me either way. All I have planned is watching basketball and ordering pizza. I did get a key made for you, though."

"I'm not sure yet. I still have a few things over there."

"Like I said, no big deal either way." He turns to leave the room. "I'll help you unload the other stuff when you bring it over."

"Thanks. I really appreciate it." Look at me accepting help and not being the one always helping others. It feels weird, but good.

I think he's already left the room, but his voice breaks the silence and echoes off the walls. "So, are we going to talk about last night?"

He just can't leave well enough alone. "I'd rather not. At least, not right now."

When I turn toward him, he's leaning against the door and nodding. "I can respect that...for now. Just know if you need anyone to talk to, I'm here."

Of course, I would room with someone that reminds me so much of Carlos. He definitely has our boss's personality. "I'll remember that." I only hope I won't have to go to him. Time will tell.

I watch him walk out of the room before moving to my stuff. If I unpack at the pace of a snail, I can put off going back to Del's a little longer. I have zero doubts in my mind we'll be having an awkward conversation, and I hope we come out of it as friends still.

10
devin

"ARE you sure you're not mad?" We're sitting at my sister's kitchen table with takeout bags in front of us. As terrified as I was to do it, I'm glad Lisa pushed me to talk to Delilah. I never knew she felt overshadowed by me our entire lives, and I never meant to make her feel that way.

We have two completely different personalities, how was I supposed to know? I guess as her twin I should have picked up on something, but I didn't. Always too focused on myself to pay attention to anything else. In high school my life was all about football, and once I graduated it became about music. It was something I always dabbled in, but never took seriously. I've spent the last few years getting better at playing, and writing, music so I can perform.

And during all those years Delilah felt like people used her to get to me. I can see her point, and definitely notice the patterns now that I'm looking back. The only person who didn't was Bryce and he didn't give her the time of day. Now... they are a couple and grossly in love with each other. I say that, but I know I was the same way with Lisa the last time we dated. I'm sure we'll be that way again.

"Yes," Delilah rolls her eyes. "For the thousandth time, I'm not mad."

"Good." I pull wings out of one of the bags while her and Bryce pull out the sides. "When do you think Lisa will be back?"

"I don't know, man." Bryce shrugs his shoulders before getting up to grab some plates. "She was taking some stuff over to Eric's, but she's been gone for hours. There's still a few of her things in the room so I know she'll be back."

Just the thought of her living with another person has jealousy pinging through all my nerves. I know I don't have anything to worry about. Eric made that clear, and Lisa isn't the type of person who would kiss someone while also pursuing someone else. It's something I'll have to get over, though. If there's anything I've learned about her in the short amount of time we dated, it's that she'll do what she wants. She's stubborn like that.

"How do you feel about that anyway?" Delilah eyes me skeptically.

"Fine," I croak. "Totally fine."

"Liar." She laughs before loading a plate up with food. "I know you better than you know yourself."

"You're right, but there isn't anything I can do about it."

"True," she points a wing toward me to make her point. The room is quiet for a moment aside from the movie playing quietly on the TV in the living room. "I think she's here."

"What?" Both me and Bryce look at her.

"A car just pulled up." She grins and stands.

"What are you tracking her or something? That's kind of creepy." Bryce jokes, but I wonder if she is. If that's the case, it's very creepy.

"No," my sister scoffs and heads toward the door. "I know how to listen to things other than what is directly around me. I know it's not something you have to do often, but us girls...

we are always aware of our surroundings. And I also saw her car pass by the window as she turned in."

"Can you believe that?" I point toward my sister. "She had us thinking she has some sort of sixth sense and the whole time it was because she saw her car."

"That's cheating if you ask me," Bryce chuckles, "but it wouldn't surprise me if they did have a sixth sense about each other. I think they have more of a twin bond than you do with your sister."

"You're probably right." Which if I think about it is kind of sad. You hear all these stories of twins being able to feel each other's emotions, but somehow that never happened with us. At least, not on my end. Gah, I'm such a self-centered ass.

Delilah opens the door, waiting for Lisa to make her entrance. A few moments pass before the girl I'm head over heels for walks in. Her eyes bounce between the three of us. Wide with shock and also a little scared. "Why do I feel like I'm walking into an intervention?"

"It's not that serious," my sister rolls her eyes. She's practically a professional at that. "Come eat lunch."

"Okay," Lisa drawls and sets her bag on the floor next to the door. "Is there a reason everyone is gathered around the table?"

"Aside from there being food?" Bryce deadpans. "Not really. Oh, except the part where you and Devin are in love with each other and secretly dated when you were here before."

"I'm gonna go to my room." Lisa backs away toward the hallway.

"Oh, no you don't." My sister steers her toward the table and forces her to sit in the empty chair next to me. "It's about time we all have a little chat."

Lisa leans toward me. "You could have given me some warning that you were talking to her today."

"I didn't give myself any warning, either," I whisper. "I called her as soon as you left the restaurant on impulse."

Bryce looks at us then Delilah. "They know we can hear them, right?"

"Who knows."

"So, how mad at me are you?" Lisa turns her attention to her best friend. "I deserve it. Whatever emotions you're feeling...throw them at me."

My sister lets her stew in worry for a few minutes. Taking a few bites of her chicken and wiping her hands slowly to add to the drama. All I can do is shake my head.

"Mad isn't really the right word."

Lisa's knee is bouncing a rapid rhythm. I slide my hand under the table and place it on her leg to calm her down. "Then what is."

"I don't know," Delilah shrugs, "disappointed? Hurt? I don't understand why you didn't think you could talk to me about your feelings. Or even hint at the fact you're in love with my brother."

"Woah, press on the brakes." Lisa holds her hands up. "Love is a strong word. I like your brother. Well, more than like him, but that's beside the point. I just didn't know how to talk to you. You made it clear you didn't want us to be attracted to each other, and I went off and ruined that. I betrayed your trust."

"Lisa," my sister leans closer to her. "I would have been less hurt if you had opened up to me. We're best friends. There shouldn't be any secrets between us."

"I know." Lisa puts her hands in her lap and stares at them. "This whole having people to rely on, and confide in, is new to me. Even then it was brand new. I've never had that and I was terrified it would screw everything up. I didn't want to push away the best people that had come into my life."

It's a shock to hear her talk like this. She's putting everything out in the open. Things she whispered to me in the dark. I had no idea she didn't confide in Delilah the same way. That tells me she does actually love me, but refuses to admit it.

"Please," Delilah snorts. "I don't think there's anything you could do that would push me away. Except for leave town without a reason and quit checking in frequently. I was ready to send out a search party."

"Sorry about that. I didn't know what else to do, and I didn't want to hear that he," she points toward me. "Moved on to someone else."

Okay, now I need to know something. "Am I the reason you came back?"

"Maybe a tiny part." She holds her fingers close together to show just how small. "But mostly, I missed everyone. I missed my family."

"Ah," my sister puts her hands to her chest. "That might be the sweetest thing I've heard all day."

"I'm pretty sure we had some pretty sweet moments when we talked earlier." I butt in. It's the first completely honest conversation we've had in years.

"Yeah, yeah. This isn't about you."

"Yeah, Dev," Lisa bumps into me. "It's not about you."

Bryce looks between us and the food. "If we're done declaring our undying love for our friendships, can we eat? The food is getting cold."

"Always thinking with your stomach," my sister laughs and gives him a quick peck on the cheek. It's sweet and weird. He was one of my best friends and now he's with my sister. I guess she feels the same way about me and Lisa. It's something I can understand.

"Is there enough for me?" Lisa asks. "Eric's fridge is practically empty and I'm starving."

I flinch at the sound of his name, but I know it would be

stupid to ask her to move in with me instead. We'll get there, step by baby step. We have to work toward what we once were.

"Yes, silly. I thought you'd be here when we got back." Delilah hands her a plate. "We can help you finish packing up your stuff after we eat."

"Sounds good to me." Lisa grabs some wings, vegetables, and fried pickles placing them in separate areas on her plate. It's absolutely adorable how she doesn't like her food to touch. Who knows maybe she'll even let me help her take her things over to Eric's. So, what if a small part of me wants to make sure he knows Lisa and I are together. Well, at least I think we are. That's something we'll have to discuss at some point today.

* * *

There were only a few boxes left to pack. Both of them are sitting in the back of my truck. Along with the air mattress we stopped by my parents to get. I can't believe of all the things in the house Carlos could take with him, it was the bed from the guest bedroom. If she doesn't get a new bed soon, I'm buying her one.

"You know you didn't have to bring my stuff, right?" She looking out the window toward her new home. "All of that would have fit in my car."

"I know, but I wanted an excuse to spend more time with you." I reach across the seat and put my hand over hers. "You know, since we have my sister's blessing now."

"I'm honestly shocked she is okay with us dating."

"So, we are, in fact, dating, right?" It feels dumb to ask her this, but I need to know for my own piece of mind.

"Yeah, I'm pretty sure that's what I just said."

"I know, I know. But earlier, when we had breakfast, you said you'd *consider* it."

She turns her hand over until our fingers are locked together. "You seriously thought I wouldn't want to be with you. I seem to remember being the one to instigate the kiss last night. That should have been answer enough."

"I just want to make sure we're on the same page," I sigh, already regretting what I'm about to say because I don't want to sound pathetic. "I haven't dated anyone since you left. I couldn't find it in me to do it."

"Your friends didn't give you shit about that?" The inside of the truck is only lit up by the dashboard lights, but I can see her eyebrows raise. "They seem like the types that would pressure you into finding the nearest pretty woman and pushing you toward them."

"I never said they didn't try." I grin and she squeezes my hand. "I wasn't interested."

"That's good to know."

"What about you? Did you date anyone?"

"Please," she scoffs. "Every town I visited I wanted to show you all the cool things I found."

"You could have texted me back."

"It hurt too much."

"I'm sorry about all of that. I really am." Even if I have to spend my life showing her how badly I feel about pushing her worries aside, I'll do it. The curtain for the front window is pulled back, and a shadow fills the frame. "We should probably take your stuff inside before Eric calls the cops on us."

"Yeah, you're right." She lets go of my hand and climbs out of the truck. "You grab the boxes. I'll get the mattress."

She closes the door and climbs on the tire to pull the mattress out of the bed of the truck before I'm even out. "Are you staying here tonight?"

"Probably not," she says as she heads toward the front door. "My car is still at your sister's house, and I'd like to sleep in an actual bed one more night."

I pull the boxes toward me and pick them up. "You can stay in my bed."

Lisa stops in her tracks. Shit. Maybe I shouldn't have said that. One of these days I'll stop blurting whatever comes to mind. Funnily enough, it only happens around her.

"That seems a little presumptuous considering we just started dating again."

"I mean," I scratch the back of my head. "Only if you want to. I'm not suggesting we have sex or anything. It's completely up to you."

Fuck. The stupidity keeps flowing. For all I know, she's going to dump me because I can't keep my mouth shut.

Instead...she laughs. "It's a possibility. No need to be so serious. I haven't seen you in months aside from small moments of stolen time." She sets the mattress on the sidewalk and makes her way toward me. "You are going to be sick of me before you know it."

I place the boxes on the ground and pull her toward me. My arms going around her waist, and hers around my neck. "That." I kiss one cheek. "Will" The other. "Never." My mouth meets hers and she melts into me. As much as I want to deepen the kiss, it's cold out here. Also, we have plenty of time for it later. I pull away from her. "Happen."

She rests her head on my chest and we bask in the moment. Finally, together after months apart. This time with my sister's blessing. "I sure as hell hope not."

The front door opens and Eric pokes his head out. "Is everything okay?"

Lisa lets go of me and turns around. "You gotta stop doing that."

"Doing what?" He cocks his head to the side in mock confusion.

"Walking in on me and Devin." She rushes to the mattress

and picks it up. "If you don't watch it, I'm going to think you're spying on me."

"Gross," he shakes his head and opens the door wide. "Folks are going to get nosy if you don't get inside soon."

While that might be true, I don't believe his reasoning for a second. As cool as he's been with my sister, I have a feeling he's going to be a thorn in my side. Too bad I need to keep those frustrations at bay. I won't do anything to make Lisa run again. And constantly bringing up Eric will do just that. It can't happen. Not when I just got her back.

11
lisa

"DO you need to let my sister know where you're at?" Devin asks from the driver side of the truck. There's a sack of food between us and drinks in the cupholder. "I can run you back over there to get your car."

"It's fine." I wave his words away. This drive is the opposite of the one the other night. Then I was determined to keep my focus on the darkness outsides. Anything to not fall for him again. Tonight, though...I can't stop staring at him. He's mine after all this time away. At least now I don't have to feel bad about it since we have Delilah's blessing.

"Are you sure?"

"Yeah, I'm sure she'll figure it out."

"True enough." He turns his blinker on and takes a right on the road his house is on. "I'll be surprised if she thinks you're coming back tonight."

He pulls into the driveway, goes past his parent's house and parks in front of his tiny home in the back part of the lot. We're on the outskirts of town and I think that's the only reason they allowed them to put in the tiny home. That and the fact they have a huge piece of property. I see his dad move away from the kitchen window. "What are your parents going to think about this? They'll won't just see me as your sister's friend."

The belly laugh coming from him is a little ridiculous. I don't think my question warrants all that. He turns the truck off, reaches over, and grabs my hand. "Apparently, they've known about us this entire time."

"What?" I shriek. Devin shushes me. "How the hell did they know?" My voice is a fierce whisper. I'm mortified.

"Well," Devin grabs my hand and walks me toward his door. He unlocks it and pushes it open. The crickets chirping the soundtrack to our night. "When my dad came by here the other night and chewed my ass out for acting like an idiot, he let on that they knew the whole time."

"Why didn't they say anything?" It feels like a pretty big secret to keep considering how close I am with Delilah.

"He said it wasn't their place." He closes the door behind us and turns on a light. Setting the bags of food on the table, he pulls a chair out for me.

This feels natural. Like old times when we'd come here after I got off work. We'd talk for hours on end and he'd write music. There were so many times we'd still be awake when the sun came up. I really have missed this.

"That was nice of them...I think." I sit down and slide my chair toward the table. The scratch of wood against the flooring is loud in the mostly quiet home.

He sits across from me and pulls the food out of the bag. It's honestly ridiculous how much fast food I've eaten this week, and I need to do better. That's a problem for another day, though.

"It was. They didn't want to make things awkward for any of us." Unwrapping his food, he shrugs. "At times, though, I think it would have made things easier for us. Everything would have been out in the open."

"And your sister would have felt betrayed because we didn't talk to her about it ourselves." Sighing, I lean back. "I think that's what made things different this time around. She knows and gave us her blessing. Even if she feels like it might be weird sometimes."

This conversation is taking me back to the last time I was here. When I walked out on Devin and left Asheville behind. I had almost gotten caught leaving the house by Delilah. It was never an issue before, but when our hours coincided, it was harder to get out without her questioning things. I told him then that we needed to tell Delilah. We needed to come clean, but he didn't want to. He didn't think she needed to know, and it wasn't any of her business.

"Things have definitely worked in our favor this time." He takes another bite. "We'll try to keep from making out in front of her so she isn't freaked out."

Of course, that's where he goes with it. Men, I shake my head and finish my food. Although, I'd be lying if I said my mind hasn't gone there as well. Especially when he's being sweet. That's something I don't see from guys our age often.

"So, are you doing music full time?" I can't believe I'm just now asking him this. It didn't come up in our other interactions because of the all the stuff going on.

The laugh that bellows out of him is loud and self-deprecating. There's a twinge of wishful sarcasm. "I wish. I still have to work at the construction site." He takes a drink of his soda. "Not for long, though. If we can get discovered, then goodbye heavy machinery, hello center stage."

"I hope that comes true for you one day." And I do. He's talked about it for as long as I've known him. That's a bridge we'll have to cross when we get there. Assuming we're still together then.

"Of course, it will." He places his hand on mine. "You'll be right by my side."

I could argue with him right now, but we're in a good place. We just became a couple again, with no fear holding me back. It's a fight I really don't want to start. Not now, anyway.

"What time do you need to go to bed? I don't want to keep you up since you have to be up early for work." A change of subject. That's what will keep any arguments from happening. Maybe he'll even forget.

He sets his food down and stands before coming to my side of the table. Holding his hand out, he waits for me to place mine in his. I can't help but wonder what he has planned.

I let him pull me up. The chair legs scratch against the floor and it falls backward with the effort. "Don't worry about that." He nods toward the chair. "Or what time I should go to bed. This is my first night with you all to myself. I'm not wasting it."

Well, that escalated quickly. This isn't exactly what I had in mind when I asked the question, but I'm not going to stop wherever this leads. "You realize we don't have to rush, right? We have more than just tonight."

"Yeah, but it's been more than six months since I've held you in my arms." He pulls me toward his bed. "Tonight...I'm rectifying that."

"Oh really?" I quirk a corner of my lips. "Just holding me is all you have planned?"

He sits on the edge of his bed and waits for me to climb into his lap. My legs straddle his, and he moves his hands from mine to my lower back. Anchoring himself to me. "I guess you'll have to find out."

He leans up until his lips meet mine, and I wrap my arms around his neck. It feels odd being the person to lean down to him. He's slightly taller than me and I always have to lift up on my toes to kiss him.

Shifting my legs, I wrap them around his waist. I can feel

exactly how much he wants me, but he's letting me lead. Letting me decide how far I want to take tonight. Even though I know we should probably take things at a snail's pace, I don't want to. It's been too long.

I push away any fears and doubts I have about our future and cling to Devin. The one person who has made me feel more special than anyone else in my life.

His arms tighten against my back and pull me closer to him, deepening the kiss. His erection pressing into me through our clothes, and I move against him. He slides his hands under my shirt. The calluses on his fingers are a welcome friction against my skin. I've missed him. Missed the connection between the two of us.

Breaking the kiss, I grab the hem of my shirt and pull it over my head. His hands move to the clasp on my bra, but he pauses. "Are you sure?"

The fact he still asks even though we've had sex before is one of the things that make him so attractive. My comfort is always at the forefront of his mind.

"Yes," I whisper. It's loud in the quiet room, and I wish we had music or some sort of background noise. But the silence only elevates every movement. Every sound. Amplifies each touch we share until I'm buzzing with energy.

His fingers make quick work of my bra, and I pull his shirt over his head. Lips meet my collarbone, and I shudder as he fiddles with the button of my jeans. With his attention in two places, it's taking too long and I climb off him. "Where are you—"

The words die on his lips as I finish the task he started and push my jeans, and panties, down my legs. "Do you need help with yours?"

"Nope," he grins and stands. He rushes to take off his pants and loses his balance. He almost hits the floor, but grabs onto the bed just in time to stop the momentum.

The giggles flow out of me. I can't help it. "Are you okay?"

"Yeah," he snorts. "Thanks for the help there."

"You had it."

In two steps he's in front of me and lifting me off the ground. "I definitely have it."

"Really?" I'm still laughing.

"Uh, huh." He sets me on the bed and hovers over me. "Who's laughing now?"

Me. It's definitely me. "It's hard to take you seriously when you're trying to be all alpha-like." I wave my hand up and down to show him exactly what I'm talking about.

He lifts one of my legs and kisses along my calf, working his way to my thigh. Pausing, he looks up at me. "I bet you're taking this seriously."

Tingles follow in the wake of his lips. I most definitely am. "Keep going."

No other words are needed, and he continues along his path. I think he's about to go down on me, but he doesn't. His mouth trails up my stomach, pausing on each breast and giving both equal attention.

My entire body is squirming with anticipation. It's been so long since I've been touched like this. Touched by him. I want him to hurry up and slow down at the same time.

Devin puts an arm under me and lifts me up, moving me further up the bed. "You good?"

"Yeah."

He leans over to his nightstand, pulls the drawer open, reaches in, and grabs a small square packet. I'm on birth control, but it never hurts to take precautions.

He sits up and makes quick work of rolling the condom over his cock before placing his focus on me. His eyes are on mine and he opens his mouth to say something, but I cut him off with a kiss. We can talk tomorrow. Right now, I want him. Need him.

Our tongues dance and his free hand runs down my body, stopping between my legs. Rubbing my clit with his thumb, he thrusts a finger inside me. Pumping in and out until I'm gasping. "Now, Devin."

He slows and slides his finger out, his cock pressing against me, and I lift my hips while he pushes inside. The pressure foreign and familiar at the same time. Six months was too long to be away from him.

His lips move from mine to my jawline. Kissing his way to my ear, sucking on the lobe and whispering into my ear. "Fuck, you feel good. I've missed you so much."

"I've missed you, too." I trail my fingers along his arms, up his shoulders, and around to his back. Pulling him deeper. Doing everything I can to close the distance between us.

He moves his hand between us, rubbing me with his thumb until my legs are shaking and I'm doing everything I can to keep my orgasm at bay. It's too soon. It's been too long, and my body is on fire for him. "Come for me."

That command is all it takes. I turn and capture his lips, letting him swallow my moans while my body rides the waves of pleasure. He follows soon after and collapses on the bed next to me. "Sorry."

He lifts up on one elbow and looks down at me. "For what?"

"That being so fast."

Lifting his free hand, he rubs my cheek with his thumb. "I wouldn't have lasted much longer, either. Besides, we both missed each other."

"You're right," I lean into his touch before glancing at the clock beside his bed. Shit. It's later than I thought. "We should probably get some sleep. Especially if you expect me to get up at the ass crack of dawn to get my car."

"Fine." He gives me a quick kiss. "Let me find something for you to wear and we'll clean up."

"Okay." I head toward the bathroom and hear drawers opening and closing.

There's a knock on the door. "I have a t-shirt and sweats for you. Do you want me to slip them in here?"

"Yeah, that's fine." The door opens far enough for him to scoot the clothes across the floor.

I slide his clothes on and splash water on my face. All the lights are off when I leave the bathroom, aside from the small lamp on his nightstand.

"I got you water." He points toward the bottle on the table. "You ready for bed?"

A yawn escapes my lips. I didn't realize I was this tired. "Yes." I climb into bed next to him. His arm curls around me, keeping me close. The weight of his arm comforting. I truly feel like I'm at home, and I hope like hell we can stay this way.

12
devin

SLEEP ELUDES ME. Maybe it wasn't a good idea to have her stay over tonight. I wouldn't trade tonight for anything in the world, though.

She's here, in my arms. The place I dreamed she'd be after all those months apart. Her soft snores fill the room, and I want that sound beside me every night. It's a pipe dream, though. There's no way I'll be able to talk her out of taking the spare room at Eric's. And honestly, it's not my place, even if it kills me on the inside. Lisa has never been one to take commands, and I'll be damned if I do anything to ruin our relationship this time around.

Everything is finally coming together. I'm playing live gigs with my friends, and I have the woman I'm pretty sure I love by my side. The only thing I need now is for someone out there to realize our talent and give us a contract.

I won't be getting any sleep tonight. I'm too amped up on emotion. Pulling my arm off Lisa, I slide to the opposite side of the bed, doing my best not to wake her. My fingers are itching for my pencil and notebook.

There's only one thing to do to shake these nerves. Lifting

the comforter, I climb out of bed, checking that Lisa is still asleep. She hasn't budged. I swear, she can sleep through anything.

My notebook is on the counter, but I don't want to turn on the light. Not with her sleeping mere feet away. Just because I'm inspired doesn't mean I need to wake her.

The bathroom may work as a place to write. Then I remember there's a small, dim light above the stove. Grabbing my notebook and pencil, I click the light on. Standing isn't ideal, but it's the only way I'll see the paper.

My pencil moves across the page with speed. Everything I'm feeling in this moment scrawled across the lines. Love, fear of losing that love, and random thoughts jotted down. I don't know if I'll be able to make sense of this in the morning, but I know I need to get it out of my head.

I haven't been paying attention to the time and my alarm blares loudly in the small house. Rushing over, I tap the button to turn it off. It's too late, though.

"Morning," Lisa stretches her arms above her. "I think."

"Good morning." I lean down and kiss her on the forehead. "You can sleep longer while I get ready if you want."

Her only answer is a nod, and I pull the covers up as her eyes drift shut. There's no reason for her to be awake unless she wants to be. And I know her. She doesn't do well with mornings. It's one of the reasons she loves working at the bar. They don't open until lunch which gives her time to get her sleep in.

I head back toward the kitchen and close my notebook. Grabbing a coffee pod out of the drawer, I place it in the coffeemaker, starting it before taking a shower. I'm going to need so much caffeine today.

With that set, I go to the bathroom. I can't believe I've stayed up this long. Even when I've been inspired before, I've never stayed up all night writing lyrics. Not that they'll make sense, but they are a start.

The room fills with steam after I turn on the water. My favorite thing about this house is it doesn't take long for the water to warm. Unlike when I lived in the house with my parents. It felt like it took forever to get the water lukewarm. Plus, I have my own space and my parents won't walk in without knocking.

They respect my space just like I respect theirs. I guess it makes more sense now why they didn't say anything to Delilah about me and Lisa. Even though they love both of us, they knew I needed to be the one that said something to her.

Quickly, I undress and step into the hot stream of water. My brain is going in a million different directions thanks to my lack of sleep. All I can hope for work today is that it's an easy one, and I won't have to use any of the big equipment. My level of exhaustion isn't exactly up to it.

"Devin." Lisa knocks on the bathroom door. "Are you almost done? I need to pee."

Why is she awake? I could have sworn she was asleep when I came in here. "The door's unlocked."

I'm not sure if she heard until a loud "ewww" comes from the other side of the door.

"What?" I rinse the shampoo out of my hair.

"I'm not going to the bathroom while you're in there." She doesn't have to sound so disgruntled about it.

"Give me a couple of minutes." I finish bathing and rinse off. As much as it doesn't make sense to me, I would rather her be comfortable. Turning off the water, I grab the towel and quickly dry my body before wrapping the towel around my waist. She's sitting on the edge of the bed when I walk out. "Bathroom is free now. Do you want me to make you a cup of coffee?"

"That would be great." I watch her walk into the bathroom. Her long hair a mess, and sticking up in various areas. At least she feels comfortable enough with me that she doesn't feel the need to make herself presentable after waking up before I see her. I dig through the nightstand and pull out a brush and hair tie she left so she can brush through it if she wants.

My closet, small as it is, is on the other side of my bed, and I hurry over to grab my clothes for work. If I stay undressed, there's no telling what might happen and I can't be late for work today. If I was smart, I'd call in, but I can't. I know she has to go into work at some point, too. We don't have to rush our time together anymore.

She comes out of the bathroom as I'm pouring coffee into two travel mugs. "Do you have any creamer?"

"Yeah, check the fridge," I nod behind me.

When I hear the fridge close, I slide over her cup so she can add whatever she wants. "Do you want any?"

Normally the answer would be yes. I typically need some flavoring added to my coffee, but not today. I need to feel the full impact and I know black coffee will do that for me. "No, I'm good. Thank you, through."

I glance up at the clock. Shit. We need to leave soon. I grab the lids to the coffee cups out of the drawer and hand one to her before putting it on my own.

She must notice my sudden rush because she begins grabbing her clothes and setting them in a pile on the bed when she notices the brush and hair tie. She brushes through her hair and puts it in a ponytail while I clean off the table. "Can I wear this home? It's cold outside, and I don't feel like putting my jeans back on."

"Sure." That jacket she wore over here last night is pretty thin. I hurry over to my closet and pull out the thickest hoodie I have, and hand it to her. "You can wear this, too." I grab my own jacket and slide it over my arms. "Give me a few minutes. I'm going to warm up the truck so it's not as cold."

"Thanks."

She wasn't wrong about it being cold. My house stays pretty toasty in the winter, with the heaters and insulation, but I am not prepared for the frigid air hitting me as I open the door. Well, if the coffee doesn't work in waking me up, this definitely will.

Opening the driver's side door, I put the key in the ignition and start it. The truck rumbles to life, and I adjust the temperature until the heater is on full blast. It won't take long for it to heat up. One of these days I'll upgrade to a truck with remote start. Maybe that will be my first big purchase if, no... when, I make it in music.

When I walk back inside, Lisa is wiping down the counter where we made coffee. It's' natural her being here, and I love seeing her at ease in my space. As much as I wish she was staying with me, I also know this space isn't big enough for the both of us. It's crowded with only me most days with the instruments I have tucked away in the corner under the TV. There isn't much storage. That will be another thing I upgrade soon. I need a bigger space. When I got this place, I was settled into being a bachelor for a while. I didn't need to have anything huge. Then I met Lisa, and I knew I wanted us to be end game.

I move behind her and wrap my arms around her waist. She leans into me and sighs. "Do we have to be responsible adults today?"

Chuckling, I shake my head. "I wish. I could spend all day with you."

"Same," she laughs. "But we have to work to get food and all that stuff. It's a good thing I love my job. Thought, I'm nervous about bartending."

Another glance at the clock and I wince. I'm going to be

late if we don't leave soon. "We need to go, but I didn't know you were going to be a bartender."

She reaches for her bag, but I beat her to it and grab it before heading to the door. She follows, but remains silent until we're inside the truck. "Carlos and Angie asked me about it when they hired me. They think I'll be good at it."

"You would be," I agree, and back down the driveway before turning onto the road. "You love talking to people, and you'll be able to do that more behind the bar than in any other position there. Plus, I know for a fact you'll get good tips."

"I hope so. I'm just nervous about remembering what all the drinks are. They had me watching what happens back there, and I think I can actually do it. I just have to go to some bartending classes to get my license."

That will mean getting to spend less time with her, but I won't hold her back if this is what she wants to do. And if the off chance we start traveling more places with the band, it's something we'll need to revisit. I can't chance losing her again. Not when I just got her back.

"Don't be nervous. I'm sure Carlos and Eric had their own little cheat sheets to remember drink combinations until they got the hang of it. Besides, you can't compare yourself to them. They've been doing this a while."

"You're right." She reaches her hand across the seat and places it on my knee. "It's just new and scary. You know, probably better than anyone, that it takes me a while to get adjusted."

She's not wrong. When we dated the first time, it was like pulling teeth to get her to let her guard down. She always had one foot out the door, ready to run, in case she got hurt. I don't blame her, though. All the issues with her mom, and not feeling like she was safe will do that to you. I can't imagine growing up without supportive parents and family members.

It makes me cherish them that much more, even when they do things to drive me nuts.

"You've got this." I turn onto the street where my sister lives. I would take her to her new place, but this is where her car is. "And if you need someone to help you practice drinks, I can always help."

"You don't drink anything besides beer."

"Neither do you."

"Actually, I've found I like variations of martinis."

Huh, that's new. It must be something she picked up while she was away. "You'll have to show me some of them."

I pull up to the curb at my sister's house and put the truck in park. Bryce's car is parked next to Lisa's, and it's weird seeing it there. My shy, sweet sister found the person who adds to her happiness, and is moving forward in their life together. I hope like hell Lisa and I can do that eventually, even if I'm making music professionally.

"I guess I should go." Lisa pulls the door handle of the truck, cracking it just enough to let the wintry air inside.

"Are you going to stay here a bit, or head home?"

"I'll probably go home. I don't want to wake your Del."

"Good point. She's grouchier than you in the mornings." Except this morning. She seems to be in a really good mood, and I'd like to think I'm part of the reason.

Before she exits the truck, she slides close to me giving me a quick peck on the cheek. "I have the coffee to thanks for less anger toward the morning. Thank you for that." She pushes the door open and climbs out of the truck. "I hope you have a good day at work. Maybe I'll see you later?"

"For sure. I'll probably come by the bar when I get off."

"See you then." She grabs her stuff and the coffee cup and closes the door.

I watch her run to her car, unlock the door, and slide in. I could have used that moment to tell her I think I'm in love with her. But she already has one thing shaking up her work life, I don't want to add anything that can cause her stress outside of that. And those few words would do that. There's no telling what she would do with the information. Tell me she feels the same way about me? Or, take off again? It could go either way, and I'm not willing to chance that. Besides, we're still new despite being in a relationship before.

Sighing, I pull away from the curb. My brain is too tired to work through all the "what ifs" and I need to get to work. It needs to be an easy day, but it's going to be a good one before I got to spend the morning with my favorite person.

13
lisa

I'M SITTING in the driveway of Eric's. I'm mean...my house. I'm not sure what to do when I get to the door. Do I knock, or use my key? This probably would have been better to do at normal hour instead of at barely seven in the morning. Who knows if Eric is even awake. I don't want to be the reason he gets up at a time he isn't used to. I know he's here because I pulled in next to his car.

My only other option is to sit in the car and wait until it's not so early. Except my heater doesn't work all that well, and it's cold. Not exactly the best combination of things. Screw it. If I wake him up, so be it. We'll figure out how to work around it as the days go on.

Turning off the car, I pull the key out of the ignition. I grab my bag and the coffee cup before opening the door. Thank God Devin gave me his hoodie. The little cardigan I was wearing last night is not enough for the early mornings in winter. I bump my door closed and weave between our cars to get to the walkway.

My steps are rushed as I approach the door. The wind is picking up speed and I have a feeling it's going to be a very cold day. One of the days I'll remember to check the forecast before I may any sort of plans so I can be prepared, but today is not that day. I set my coffee on the ground and shuffle through the keys on my keyring. You'd think it would be easy to find the one for the door, but it's not. I have a key to Delilah's house, the bar, my car, and even some old keys from places I've stayed in the past. The problem is most of them look the same, aside from my car key. I need to go through and get rid of the ones I'm no longer using. Or get keys made in different colors so I know which ones belong to the correct doors.

My eye catches a newish looking one, and I slide it into the door. My fingers tremble from the wind and I turn. Please be the right key. The lock clicks and I celebrate the victory with a little dance. Normally, I'm not this awake in the mornings, but something about waking up in Devin's bed and the added benefit of coffee has my mood soaring.

I turn the knob and push the door open before grabbing my coffee and walking inside. Sweet, sweet warmth. Pushing the door closed behind me, I reach back and lock it. It feels strange not being in Del's house, but it's something I know I'll get used to with time.

The house is quiet as I make my way down the hall toward my room. Eric's door is shut tight, and I'm guessing he's still asleep. It's not like he's out and about without his car. I open my door, and grimace at the amount of work that needs to be done to put things away. I planned on taking a small nap, but forgot to blow up the air mattress before I left last night. The noise would wake Eric, and that's the last thing I want to do. It would put me at the top of the shitty roommate list.

Setting my bag on the floor, I pull out my phone and head back toward the living room. Putting this stuff away is a problem for later. I still need to figure out what furniture I need to get in order to fit my meager belongings. It's something I can't wait to do, though. Buying stuff for my room will make it feel like mine, and also offer a permanence. A step in building a life here. The one thing that excites and terrifies me all at the same time. I don't think anyone realizes just how much. I'm pretty good at fake it 'til you make it in that regard.

Just as I'm settling in on the sofa, with room idea images on my phone screen, the lock on the front door clicks. What the hell? Eric said I was the only other person with a key. I slowly get off the couch and rush toward the kitchen. It takes me three drawers until I find something I could potentially protect myself with.

Tiptoeing toward the door, I wait until the door opens so I can get a look at who is coming through. The door opens in so it gives me additional cover. Slowly, it opens and it takes a few seconds for someone to emerge through the gap, and I can't see who it is.

I jump out with the knife held in front of me at whoever my would-be attacker is. Eric stumbles back and puts his hands in the air. "Woah, there. It's just me."

"Oh my God." I drop the knife and cover my mouth with my hands. "I am so sorry." And I am. He's probably thinking I'm bonkers and wants me to move out immediately after this little display. "I thought you were in your room asleep. I could have hurt you."

"First off, you probably shouldn't try to attack a person who is coming into the house." He picks up the knife. "Secondly, you're gonna want to take the blade cover off the knife before using it." He walks past me and sets the knife on the high bar that separates the entry way from the kitchen. "And lastly, I doubt a burglar would be breaking in with a key."

I. Am. Mortified. It's a good thing nobody else was here to witness that little scene. They would never let me live it down. "How was I supposed to know?"

"I mean," he shrugs, "it's common sense."

"I really am sorry." I walk back toward the living room, and sit on the sofa. "Being up earlier than normal and all the coffee I've had this morning has me jittery."

"It's okay." He laughs and sits on the opposite side of the sofa. "At least I know you'll come to the rescue if there's ever an intruder."

"Not that I'd be much help since I couldn't even tell it had a cover on it." I reach for a blanket on top of the sofa, but he doesn't have one. It's so instinctive since Delilah has them on hers. We'll have to remedy that. If only so I have something when I'm in here. We should also probably bring in some sort of arm chair. "Where were you, anyway?"

"Running."

"On purpose?" That's insanity to me.

"Yeah, I get up and run every morning. Unless it's raining. That's the only time I don't."

"But, why? And, how after working so late?" I will never understand people who don't need hours and hours of sleep to function. The few hours I got last night will most likely be a problem for me later in the day. I really need to work a nap in.

He stands and heads to the kitchen. Grabbing a bottle of water, he cracks the lid and takes a drink. Finally, he answers me. "Running helps me clear my mind. It's why I ran track in high school. And I'm one of the few people I know that is able to get up early with little sleep. I don't get tired and I can still keep going." When he notices the death glare I'm shooting at him, he shrugs. "What can I say? It's a gift."

"It's not fair is what it is."

"I take it you're not a morning person?"

"Not even close. That's why I like working at the bar. They don't open before ten, and I can sleep."

And that is the main reason I've always worked at bars. I'm a night owl by nature. I never understood the whole early bird thing, and I don't care to.

"So." He sits on the sofa again and leans against the arm rest. "Where were you last night? Being a party animal?"

"I was with Devin." I hope he doesn't try to give me his be careful speech. I know what I'm doing, and I want to be with Devin. I appreciate the concerned friend approach, but I have no need for it.

"I'm glad y'all are working it out." My mouth hangs wide open and I'm taken back. Did he really just say that? I'm almost tempted to reach across the sofa and feel his forehead. Any other interaction where Devin is concerned has been approach with caution. Now he's all in?

"Really?"

"Yeah. I shouldn't have stuck my nose where it didn't belong. I barely know the guy aside from the fact he's Delilah's brother and plays music at the bar." He grins and picks up the remote. "I'm perfectly capable of admitting when I'm wrong."

Clapping my hands together, I laugh. "Congrats. You are one of the few people I know who can do that. Even Carlos has a hard time saying someone else is right."

"You'd be surprised. Caroline and David have changed him a lot." He turns on the TV and flips through the channels. It's Monday morning so it's mostly news shows, and I do my best to avoid news at all costs because it can put me in a bad place. "Not in a bad way, but I'm shocked you haven't noticed."

I have noticed. Joy that he's found someone who makes him happy fills me. He became a sort of honorary father figure for me, or at the very least favorite uncle. I'm not sure what I would have done without him talking Angie into giving me a chance at the bar. Even though everyone sees him as a gruff and grumpy person, he was never that way toward me. It's one of the reasons I found everyone's attitude toward him so weird.

"What time do you go in today?" I may need his help when I get back if I can find a bed frame for stupid cheap.

"I close tonight. So later this afternoon."

"Oh." Well, there goes my plans for getting him to help me. He'll be at the bar before I get off.

"Why, what do you need?"

"Help getting a bed if I can find one."

"I'm guessing you go in around lunch." I nod and he continues. "Tell, you what. How about I get cleaned up and we can go to the store. I know a few places that have the bed and frame for crazy cheap. If we don't have time to set it up before you leave for work, I can do it if you tell me where you want it."

"I'm game for that." At this point I'll do anything because I don't want to sleep on an air mattress if I don't have to. They aren't comfortable at all. "I also need to jump in the shower."

"Meet back in here in thirty minutes?"

I calculate the time it'll take me and nod. "Meet you then. Thank you."

"No worries." He stands and holds his hand out to help me up. "What are friends for?"

He's right. I've spent so long keeping people at an arm's length, other than Delilah, that I forgot what it's like to have people you can count on.

* * *

It's definitely a Monday, and every one of the patrons coming into the bar feels the same way it seems. Almost all the tables in the dining area are full and people have moved over into the area with stage for more room even though there isn't live music tonight. We close at midnight tonight, and I can't help but wonder if I'll be asked to stay to help out. It's not a huge deal, but I'm anxious to get home and see my new bed.

We didn't have time to set it up, but Eric assured me he'd get it done before he comes in. Which should be any minute. Someone texted me earlier, but I've been running around so much I haven't had time to check who it was. Only one hour. That's all I have to last before going home.

I'm walking back to the host stand when Carlos motions me over. He's about to leave for the day. Something about extra practice for Caroline's son. He really has become the all-around family man. I approach the bar to see what it is. Please don't be a request to stay later. Aside from the bed, I need to get some sort of sleep tonight.

"Whatcha need, Boss Man?"

He rolls his eyes. "I really wish you wouldn't call me that."

"But it's what you are, and I think it fits."

"Fine, I'll let it slide." He waves away the annoyance. "You better be happy you're my favorite."

Well, I'm glad to know I'm his favorite even though I already knew that. A crowd of people come through the door. Shit. "But for real, what did you need?"

He glances toward the door and winces, knowing he's causing a backup of service. "I left a list of bartending schools on the desk in the office. Most of them take place in the evenings and some on the weekends. Decide which one you want to go to, and we'll send over the payment and get it set up."

The customers at the door are getting antsy. I need to get to them before they decide they want to go somewhere else. "I'll look it over when I get off."

He looks like he wants to make another request. No doubt wondering if I can work a bit later, but I head toward my station before he can. "Welcome to Out of the Ashes. How many are in your party?"

I glance behind me to see if there are any long tables to put them at in the dining area. They have six people in their group. Luckily there's another group leaving. I wave down one of the bussers. He gets to work cleaning the table, and turn back to the party patiently waiting. "It'll be just a few moments."

The man in front nods his acceptance and I count down the minutes until I can leave. Once the table is cleared, I show the group to their seats and let them know someone will be by to take their order. Devin is standing at the stand when I return. "Hey."

"Hey back." He looks me over. "You look stressed."

Damn. I wonder how rough I actually look if it's noticeable. "It's been…a long day."

"When do you get off?"

I glance at the clock over the bar. "In about thirty minutes."

"Cool." He glances behind him to make sure he isn't holding up a line. "We get food and hang out after you get off if it'll help."

"That would be great." I'm making sure my area is cleaned up before Delilah comes in to relieve me. "Crap. Actually, I have to run to the store. Eric helped me pick up a bed before I came in, and I forgot to get sheets."

His entire body stiffens and I wonder what I did to upset him. "I can get you some and meet you at your place."

"Really?" He truly is the best. "It's a queen size. I can bring us some wings for dinner. If that's okay with you."

"Sounds good. Any certain color you want me to get?"

"Nope. Surprise me." As soon as the words leave my lips, I realize it might be a mistake. What if he comes back with something horrible? Though, the bedding he has isn't horrible.

He leans over the stand and kisses me on my cheek. I'm not a huge fan of PDA, but this is okay. It's not like we're making out at my job. "I'll see you in a bit."

He really is the best guy. How many boyfriends would offer to buy bedding for you?

Not long after he leaves Eric and Delilah come in for their shift. "Hey, did you get the bed set up?"

"I sent you a picture. It's ready to go."

"Thanks, you're the best." I give him a quick hug. To Delilah, I whisper, "good luck tonight. It's been hectic."

"Looks like it." She takes a peek around the corner to the dining area. "Get out of here. I've got the rest of this."

I clean up the area underneath and wave. I'm about to walk out the front, but remember the paper Carlos told me about, and the wings.

I walk to the back asking Patrick to make a couple of orders for me and get the paper. Nerves wrack through me because despite my comfort level with Devin, tonight is the first time he'll be visiting a space that is my own.

14
devin

I'M STANDING in the bedding aisle, and I have no idea which sheets to get Lisa. She's not a fan of pastels, but she doesn't like dark colors either. Why did I offer to do this? And why didn't she call me to help her find a bed. Even though I know Eric is only her friend, it's still a hard pill to swallow that he helped her pick one out. That feels like a couple thing to do.

I'm completely out of my element. I thought we'd be able to pick back up where we left off. We have in a way, but she has her own space, and I'm not sure how that will work. Before we always went to my house, or drove the backroads. Now...I don't know where I fit in.

Someone walks up behind me and taps my shoulder. "You look like you're in deep thought."

Angie is standing behind me, waiting for me to say something. "I offered to pick up some sheets for Lisa, but I have no idea which ones she'll like."

"Go with the purple."

"Are you sure?" I've never seen her wear purple so I'm not even sure if she likes the color.

Nodding she grabs the package of sheets off the shelf. "Definitely. She'll love them."

"Thanks. I just don't want to screw things up again." Shit. I clamp my mouth shut. "Sorry, I don't think us dating before was common knowledge."

"To most people probably not, but I always know what my employees are going through." She puts the sheets in my hand. "And from what Carlos told me, it was a busy day at the bar, she's going to be exhausted. If you want my advice, get her some flowers, chocolate, and maybe even some alcohol."

"Okay, I'll do that." It's kind of weird to be getting advice from her, but I'll take it.

"Good luck." She turns to leave, but stops. "Oh, I almost forgot what I was coming to tell you. Stella got a couple of gigs added to the calendar. I'll send you an email with the information. I think some of the members from Crooked Halo will be stopping by too."

"Seriously? When? Is it a night we're playing?" Please say yes. It was so cool coming on stage before them, but I didn't get a chance to meet them afterward. I had to be the responsible one and get my friends home.

"I'll send you the details, but you'll definitely get to play in front of them."

"Awesome." And it will be as long as I can keep my shit together. I wonder if there's any way Lisa can be off the clock that night. I have a feeling I'm going to need her support more than ever. "I'll, uh, see you later then."

She waves and walks away. She may be one of the coolest people I know. I rush around the store to gather the rest of the stuff she suggested. I could be cliche and get a bouquet of roses, but I don't want to do that. I pick through all the flowers and grab a colorful bunch of daisies. She'll love these.

I weave through people to get to the self-checkout. There's

only one place I'm excited to be now. I need to stop letting Eric get under my skin and focus on Lisa.

* * *

I pull up to the curb in front of Lisa's house at the same time a car pulls into the driveway. I'm not sure how we managed that, but at least neither of us is waiting on the other. Turning off my truck, I reach over to the passenger seat and grab the bags. Fear that she may not actually like the sheets hits me. I don't know why it feels like a big decision because in the grand scheme of things it's not. They are sheets for crying out loud. I even went above and beyond. There's a comforter a few shades darker than the sheets I bought.

Opening the door, I get out and come close to dropping the bags. Shifting my grip, I hold tight to them as I bump the door shut. Lisa is getting out of her car as well, and smiles when she turns around and sees me. "Hey, I figured you would have beat me home. I almost forgot to have Patrick make the wings so had to wait a tiny bit longer."

"It's all good. I actually ran into Angie while I was at the store." I make my way toward her. "I have some potentially big news."

"Really? I can't wait to hear about it. She moves the bags of food to her other hand. "Let me help you."

"I've got it." I reach for the bags in her hand. "Give me those so you can open the door."

She looks at my two full hands and raises her eyebrows. "How are you going to carry them? With your teeth?"

"If I need to." Always so stubborn. One of these days that's liable to bite her in the ass.

She turns toward the walkway and heads toward the front door. Okay then, that answers that. There's nothing left for me to do except follow after her. What I don't think she realizes is I would follow her anywhere. If it wouldn't have raised suspicions, and I knew where she was going, I would have gone after her when she left.

The door is unlocked and open before I make it to her. "Hurry it's cold."

Stubborn and bossy. I definitely know how to pick them. "I'm coming, I'm coming." I step sideways to fit through the door without hitting the bags. She closes the door behind me.

"I'm going to get these put on plates." She lifts the bags in her hand. "You can set those down in my room. I'll get them put on later."

"Okay, I'll be back in a minute." As I make my way down the short hallway, I can hear doors opening and closing. I bet she still hasn't found her way around the kitchen yet. It works for me because it gives me some time.

Setting the bags on the floor, I pull the sheets out. The bed is set up against the wall closest to the door and I get to work taking the packaging off. I slide the corners of the fitted sheet over the mattress and follow with the flat sheet. I don't know if she likes them, but it comes in the set so I might as well put it on.

Next up is the comforter and I throw it over the bed, straightening the edges until they are the same length. I look around for pillows to slip the cases on, but I don't see any. I didn't think to ask if she had pillows. That's something I can pick up tomorrow if I need to.

More bangs come from the kitchen, and I'm not sure how much time I have left. Do I take the rest of this to the kitchen? Or do I set it out in here?

"Devin?" Footsteps approach from the hall. Shit. I'm about to have my mind made up for me.

Grabbing the chocolate candy, wine and flowers from the other bag, I hold them in front of me. She opens the door and gasps. "These are for you." I hold them out in offering.

"Thank you." She rushes between my arms and throws hers around my neck. "How did you even know?"

"I had an inside hint from someone." I send up a silent thanks to Angie. Her suggestions were definitely the right call.

She lets go of me and turns toward the bed. "You didn't have to make the bed for me. I planned on doing it after you leave."

Well, now I know she doesn't want me to stay the night. Which is fine. We can't smooch all of our time together. We would get tired of each other. She'd get tired of me because I love spending every moment I can with her, and it's better now since we can be out in the open together.

"It was no trouble at all. Just one more thing I could take off your plate. Do you have any pillows? I looked for some to slip into the pillowcases, but didn't see any."

"Yeah," she shrugs. "I have some, but they are probably in one of the boxes." She grabs my hand and pulls me toward the door. "Don't worry about that now. We need to eat before the food gets cold."

I let her lead me to the living room. There isn't a kitchen table. It makes sense for when it was only one person living here, but now that there are two maybe it's something they should invest in. It's not my business, though. The reminder is something I'll have to keep on repeat about their living arrangement even though it's going to be so hard.

"Thank you for the food. I love the wings there."

"I know," she grins. "That's why I got them." She pushes one of the plates on the coffee table toward me. "So, what is the big news Angie told you?"

Fear over actually telling her consumes me. It's one of those counting your chickens before they've hatched situations. I mentioned it, though, and I need to tell her. She'll be one of my biggest cheerleaders because that's the type of person she is.

"You know the band Crooked Halo? The band that performed at the bar on New Year's?"

"Yeah. I mean I head off them before. They're like an overnight success or something."

If people only realized how many years it takes to become an overnight success, it would be a miracle. But I'm not going to blame Lisa for not knowing how long Crooked Halo has been performing. "Yeah, they're kind of a big deal. But that's not the exciting part."

"Which is the part I want to know." She takes a bite of her chicken. Her eyes locked on me until I answer.

"Well, Angie told me Crooked Halo will be coming to the bar and watching some of the performances."

She tilts her head to the side, confused. "I thought y'all were the only performers?"

It would be nice if we got a little more time to have the stage just for us, but like I told Angie, we need more bands if we're going to draw in more people.

"That was only until Stella could find more bands and singers. Apparently, she's done that." Though, I'm shocked at how quick she was about it. I thought for sure we'd have another month.

She takes another bite, chewing as she thinks through everything I said. The silence of the room is deafening, and I wish she had turned on the TV or something. Anything to fill the void.

"I'm confused." She tucks a stray piece of hair behind her ear. "What is the purpose of them coming to the bar? Are they looking to sign the band or something like that? If that's the case, they should've just done a battle of the bands."

All very good questions and ones I wish I would've asked Angie when she was standing in front of me at the store.

"From the way Angie was talking, it sounds like they are looking for new talent. And you're right, battle of the bands would be the best way to do it, but they are a lot of work. I don't think Angie or Stella want to go through all of that."

"But wouldn't that bring more traffic to the bar, and more focus on the live music?"

"Probably. But it could be scheduling reasons with Crooked Halo. I'm surprised they are coming back out here since they are on tour."

She grabs another piece of chicken. "Wouldn't it be cool if they're looking for another band to go on tour with them?"

"It's kind of what I'm hoping for." This is the kind of opportunity bands kill for. Add in the fact they're coming to this little hole in the wall town, and I feel like my chances have skyrocketed. Hell, the only reason they are coming here is because I've heard they are close to Stella's cousin and her fiancé. All the cool stuff happens to everyone else.

"Oh." What does she mean *oh*? I've told her so many times that this is what I want to do with my life. "I'm sure you and the band will do great. I have zero doubts about that."

"I'll have more information when Angie emails me, but I'll have to rehearse more with the band. And write more music. We can't keep playing the same songs over and over." The lyrics I wrote this morning are waiting for me to come back to them. Not staying the night here is probably a good idea. If only so I can work on that song, and get some actual sleep.

"I can't wait to see what you come up with." She leans over and kisses me on the cheek. "When you get on the stage in front of that band, I'll be there supporting you. Front and center."

She might not seem very excited about the prospect of me going on tour, but at least she'll be there for me. The rest of the details we can work out if they happen. No, not if, when.

Talking about it like it's a done deal is exactly what I need to keep my head in the game.

"That means a lot." I scoot closer to her and pull her into my lap. "I'll have to get with the guys so we can figure out a schedule. Mostly because I want to spend as much time with you as I can."

"It's fine." She leans her head back. "I'm sure some nights I'll be working the late shift, and I'm about to start bartender training. Fingers crossed we can work around both things." Snuggling into me, she sighs, "I could fall asleep right here."

"Me too." Picking up the remote off the coffee table, I turn on the TV. "Want to find something to watch?"

"Sure. Though I don't know what all Eric has on here. I haven't had much time to explore the options, and he always has it on some kind of game."

I click through the channels. "I'll stop on the first show that's not on commercial." It happens to be a crime show. She slides off me, and we lay on the couch. The show is a rerun I've seen too many times, but it's better than letting my thoughts go wild with her lack of enthusiasm over the band.

Soft snores come from beside me. It didn't take her long to pass out. Angie definitely wasn't lying about it being busy if she's asleep by nine. As much as I'd like to stay right here, I need to get home.

Moving as gently as possible, I climb out from behind her. There isn't a blanket on the couch, so I hurry to her room and grab one I saw on top of one the bags of stuff she still needs to put away.

After laying it over her, I grab one of the napkins off the table and search through the kitchen drawers for a pen. It takes a few tries to find the junk drawer, but I know it's some-thing everyone has in their house.

I scribble a note on the napkin and lay it down on the coffee table. Leaning down, I press a soft kiss to her forehead.

She moves, but doesn't wake up. I grab the paper plates, take them to the kitchen, and throw them in the trash can.

Not saying goodnight sucks, but I don't want to wake her. Especially if her nights are about to be as long as mine. We're going to need all the sleep we can get. There's only one more thing I need to do when I get home, and I hope like hell it doesn't keep me up all night.

15
lisa

MY BODY IS BOUNCING up and down. For a second, I think I'm dreaming, but my eyes pop open and Eric is hovering over me. "Wake up, Lisa."

"Ugh, why are you so close?" I push him away from me. "And where is Devin?"

Eric picks up something from the coffee table. "He, uh, left a note."

The TV is still playing in the background, but instead of the show I was watching with Devin, it's informercials. I loathe those with every fiber of my being. My mom would spend all night buying shit off the TV she was never going to use, and fail to do anything to take care of my basic needs. Those actions were the first of many where she showed me just how little she cared for me. It only got worse throughout the years.

I grab the remote from the coffee table and press the power button with more force than necessary before tossing it on the sofa. Eric is staring at me like I have two heads. "You okay there?"

"Yeah, sorry. I just hate those programs." I pull my legs

under me on the sofa. I'm not sure what time it is, but it has to be late if Eric is home. "You said he left a note."

"Here you go." He hands it to me before standing and walking toward the hallway. "I wasn't going to wake you up, but you'd probably be more comfortable in your bed." He takes a step back. "Let me know if you need anything."

"I will, thanks." I wait until he turns the corner, and is out of sight before lifting the napkin to my face. It's creative, I'll give him that.

You looked so peaceful, and I didn't want to wake you. Call me in the morning and let me know what your schedule is for the rest of the week. Maybe we can grab dinner before our schedules are too busy. Miss you already.

A part of me wants to text him and thank him for the note, but the other part knows that probably isn't a great idea. Not because he wouldn't welcome it, but because he's most likely asleep. At least normal people are.

Pushing the blanket off me, I stand and grab it. The note is still clutched in my hand, and I head to the kitchen to get a bottle of water. I look around for our food mess, but I'm assuming he cleaned it up before leaving. It feels like something he would do.

My feet drag as I make my way to my room. The door is still open, and I close it behind me. After setting the napkin on the dresser, I turn toward my bed and fall into it face first. I don't even feel like digging through my stuff for the pillows. I'm too tired, and that is now a tomorrow problem.

My butt vibrates as my phone goes off. There's only one person it can be, but I don't feel like talking. I'll call him in the morning like the note says. I pull the phone out of my pocket and toss it somewhere above me on the bed.

With any luck tomorrow will be a slow day. I don't know if I can handle another day like this. I forgot how busy it gets, especially since it's the only bar in town.

Eric should have let me sleep on the couch because now a million thoughts are flashing through my mind and making sleep next to impossible. I keep my eyes closed hoping I'll doze off in the meantime.

* * *

"How do you feel about starting bartending training tonight?" Carlos leans against the bar and awaits my answer.

"But the one I chose doesn't start until next week." Tonight, is a little soon, and I haven't mentally prepared myself for that kind of pressure.

"I know, I know." He waves his hands toward me, already knowing I'm about to spiral, and trying to get me to calm down. "But the class you want is full. You can start tonight, or push it out to the next class."

"What all does it entail?"

He waves Delilah over to him and whispers something to her. She relieves me from the host stand and I move toward the bar so Carlos and I can talk without it being broadcast to the whole bar.

"Nothing and everything all in one?" He shrugs his shoulders. "They'll teach you what you need to know for your server certification, but they also show you how to break down and set up the bar. You'll learn how to make drinks, especially the popular ones."

"Couldn't Eric show me how to do all that and I get my certification some other way?" Yes, it's fear trying to talk me out of this, but what if I screw up. I'll be a disappointment to both Carlos and Angie. I can't believe after all these years my mom's voice is still in the back of my head telling me I'll never be good enough. But there it is, and I don't know that it'll ever change.

"He could, and you could get your certification online, but...attending a class lets you go through the entire process in one swoop. And you'll find that you develop your own little twists to some of the drinks. It's something that helps you stand out to customers, and what keeps them coming back." He puts an arm over my shoulder. "Besides, have you seen how busy we've been? There's no way Eric would have the time to teach you and work the bar at the same time."

He's right. It's not like I'm paying for the class myself. They said they would take care of it. "How long do the classes last?"

"Two weeks." His arm drops and he moves in front of me. "Four hours a day during the week, except this one runs Tuesday through Saturday. And the Saturday sessions are in the morning."

That really isn't that long, and I'm sure I'll make friends easily. I always do, and it's why they want me to be a bartender. He watches me puzzle it out in my head, and it's kind of funny. "Fine," I groan. "I'll start tonight. Will I be able to get off slightly earlier to make it to class on time?"

"Of course. We'll work it out." He pats my shoulder, and the grin on his face helps lessen the fears, at least a little. "I'll go call them now and get them your information."

"Sounds good. I'm just gonna go over there and do my job." I point toward the stand where Delilah is grinning. He doesn't have anything to say to that and he heads back to the office. "Please tell me I can do this?"

Delilah wraps me in a hug. "You've totally got this. In fact, you're going to be so good, you'll give Eric a run for his money."

"I don't want it to be a competition."

"For sure, but he's competitive in nature. It'll be friendly fun." She starts to leave my station, but turns back toward me. "By the way, how's it going rooming with him? We haven't had the chance to talk much."

"I mean, it's only been like a day," I shake my head. "We'll need groceries for sure. I don't think he actually cooks anything besides frozen food. He did wake me up after I fell asleep on the couch last night and told me to go to bed. Then it took forever to fall asleep again."

"He was playing mother hen. He's like that with literally everyone. I think it's because his mom is that way with him. Which is also why he rarely cooks. If he doesn't have frozen dinners, he usually has food his mom sends home with him."

Those few statements are a punch to the gut. I would give anything to have a mom who even cared where I was. Or actually wanted to do anything for me that didn't benefit her. "Is she a good cook?"

"Oh yeah," Del nods. "He shares some with me when he gets too much. Though, I think that'll change now that you're living there. You'll be glad for it, I promise."

"I'll take your word for it." I shoo her away and lean against the podium. All these people in my life have loving and supporting parents, even if it's just one. It makes me wonder what I did wrong. Why my mom chose to never be there for me. It's something that's plagued me for years, and it's the reason I left home as soon as I could. It wouldn't do any good to be somewhere I wasn't wanted.

My phone buzzes on the shelf beneath me. I glance toward the door to make sure nobody is walking, and turn to ensure my help isn't needed anywhere else. I pick it up and swipe open the screen.

DEVIN

Is everything okay? You didn't call this
morning.

LISA

Yeah. I slept past my alarm and had to rush
to get to work on time.

DEVIN

Cool. Want to do dinner tonight?

Damn it. I forgot we were going to figure out some dates before our schedules got busy. It slipped my mind when I agreed to start the bartending class tonight.

LISA

Actually…the bartending class I wanted
was full, but they have a spot for the one
starting tonight. I told Carlos I'd take it so I
can get started behind the bar sooner.

DEVIN

Oh, ok. Maybe this weekend after we
perform, we can grab food at one of the all-
night breakfast places.

LISA

Definitely. I'm so sorry.

DEVIN

No, it's fine. Good luck at class tonight.

LISA

Thanks.

He sounds upset. I could be reading into it wrong, but I can't help the gut feeling that I've let him down. Maybe he thinks I should have touched base with him before I decided on the class. We just started dating again, and while we've picked up where we left off in some ways…in others we're starting over. We aren't exactly at a place where we check in about decisions.

Well, not exactly. This class isn't life altering. Hearing him talk about wanting to get picked up by that band had my head in a tailspin last night. That is something that will change the trajectory of his life, and mine, if he wants me in it. But I'll be there for him. That's my job as his girlfriend. Who knows maybe his band won't get picked and it's something we won't have to worry about. If they do...I guess I'll cross that bridge when we get there.

* * *

There are five other people in this class with me. I assumed there would be more, but I have no idea because this isn't a job I ever considered before moving back to Asheville.

We spent the first half of class time going over some of the basic rules. Now we're going over how to prep a bar. I never realized how much work the bartenders do just to serve the patrons for the night. It makes sense, though. It also explains a bit more why Carlos is the way he is about keeping the bar. Him and my instructor would get along well.

Thirty minutes. That's all that's left of class after going over the bar. I keep expecting to make a drink, or even pour one. But no. All we've done is go over every little thing we can expect to find behind the bar.

Why are there so many types of shakers? I'm pretty sure Out of the Ashes doesn't have this same variety. Or, maybe they do. I haven't spent much time back there. There's never been a reason for me to. Hell, I only ever wait tables when we've been short staffed. Thank God those days are over.

I've zoned out and don't know what the instructor just spoke about. Raising my hand, I rack my brain for his name. I honestly can't remember, and I hope like hell he reintroduces himself again.

He sighs as he points to me. "Yes?"

Definitely not making a good impression tonight. Tomorrow I will do better. "Sorry, I missed what you were saying about that section."

One of the guys in class smirks at me, and I wish I could swipe it off his face. He's good looking and I have no doubt he'll make great tips when he starts tending bar, but I don't need for him to chastise me. He's a newbie, just like me.

"It's basically the sink area." He points toward it. "It can fill up fast even if it's a slow day. Your best bet is making sure the barback keeps it cleaned up. Most of the time you won't be able to manage it while making drinks for customers."

"Thanks." The word is barely audible, and I already feel like I'm letting Carlos down. My focus needs to be on point. He's paying for me to have this opportunity, and I can't fail him.

He goes over a few more things before announcing class is over. I rush to grab my bag and head toward the door. Another classmate of mine walks beside me. "Hey, don't let that guy get you down. It's a lot of information to take in."

"I'm trying not to." I stick my hand out, "I'm Lisa."

"Joan," she places her hand in mine. "It's nice to meet you."

"You too." We continue out the door into the dark parking lot. As much as I'm not in the mood for small talk, it's nice having someone walk toward the car with me. Especially at night.

I reach my car and she happens to be parked directly in front of me. "Maybe we can quiz each other on all this so we don't fail the class." She calls out as she opens her door.

She's very nice, and it may be a good idea. This whole bartending thing may be more than I can handle. "Definitely.

We can exchange numbers tomorrow before class. I plan on getting here a little early."

"Sounds good." She waves and slides into her car. At least I've managed to make a friend. With her help, I may actually figure out what I'm doing. When it comes to bartending, anyway.

16
devin

IT'S BEEN days since I've actually seen Lisa. We've talked on the phone and sent texts back and forth, but it's not the same. I thought we'd see each other more now that we have my sister's blessing, not less. Things keep getting in our way. Whether it be her bartending classes, or my band rehearsals. We can't seem to get on the same page.

I'm at the bar now, waiting on Trey and Cash to show up. This is why we always ride together. Otherwise, they're late and I'm worried about if they'll get here in time to play. The fact Lisa won't be here until we're almost done is also something that's not sitting well with me.

I've played before without her here, but now I could really use the support. Crooked Halo is going to be here in two weeks and her input on how we're doing will help ease my nerves.

My sister spots me standing outside the door. Crap. I knew I should have waited for them in the alley. She weaves through the people waiting to be seated and opens the door. "Why aren't you inside?" She rubs her arms to warm up against the winter night.

"You should probably be wearing a jacket."

"And you should be inside getting set up." She points toward the bar. "Again, why aren't you in there?"

"I'm waiting on my bandmates to pull up, so I can go to the back and let them in."

"The door is unlocked," she sighs. "I made sure of it this time before the night crowd rolled in."

"Oh." She does pay attention. Though last time she sent Lisa back there to open the door for us. Just to think if she hadn't, we wouldn't have rekindled what we once had. Though it feels different this time, and full of a chaos we didn't have when we were dating in secret.

Delilah picks up my guitar and shoves it into my chest. "So, get your ass back there and call your friends to see where they are."

"When did you get so bossy?"

"Funny." She laughs and pushes me toward the door. "I'm just trying to make it easier for you, and you're going to block the sidewalk when more people come in."

"Speaking of," I stop in front of the door before pulling it open. "Do you know if it's common knowledge that Crooked Halo will be here in a couple of weeks?"

"Not that I know of." She walks around me and opens the door. "It's not like they're playing, and they don't want the fanfare. They will be here to find new talent, and that's it."

Good to know. The bar won't be a total circus, until someone spots them and posts it on social media. Oh well, that's a problem for Angie to handle. "Thanks." I take a few steps inside. "Oh, keep an eye out for Lisa. She'll be here as soon as she's out of her class."

"I know." She throws her hands up in the air. "You act like her and I don't talk. Despite y'all being in a relationship, she's still my best friend."

Instead of saying anything else, I hightail it inside and head straight to the back. Eric waves as I pass by, and that's odd. Ever since Lisa has been back, he's done nothing but warn her away from me. Well, at least until we got together. Now...I don't know what he thinks. But his reaction to me has turned around completely. It's not a bad thing, just...weird. At least Lisa will be happy her roommate is getting along with me.

I wave back at Eric and continue to the side of the stage. Setting my guitar down, I go to the door that leads to the alley. Pushing it open, I peek outside. I don't see Trey or Cash coming down with their equipment. I swear, they can't be on time to anything unless I'm the one driving.

Pulling my phone out of my pocket, I open our group text and send them a message.

DEVIN

Where the hell are you? We're supposed to play in less than twenty minutes.

CASH

We're pulling in right now. Trey had to take his dog to the vet and they took longer than expected. Then he had to take him to his mom to watch him while we're here.

DEVIN

Trey, I'm glad your dog is better. But please hurry. We started late last week and I don't want to make it a habit.

CASH

Yes sir.

It's a valid reason for being late. But did he have to choose today of all days to get his dog checked out. He knows we play on Friday and Saturday.

Finally, I see headlights shine into the alley. I turn the handle on the outside to make sure it's actually unlocked before walking outside. My steps are quick as I make my way to the opening. Trey and Cash as jumping out of the car. The trunk is already popped open and I grab as many things as I can.

Trey unloads the backseat, and Cash gets what I couldn't. We really need a better system to carrying our instruments around. One of these days shoving them into any open area in our vehicles is going to break them, and then we'll be screwed.

"I'm sorry, Dev." Trey says as we get closer to the back door. "It's the only day the vet had open for weeks and I had to get my baby checked out."

"It's fine." I open the door and hold it for them to go through. "Y'all ready to do this thing?"

"Hell yeah," Cash yells as we carry the equipment onto the stage.

This is one thing I hope we don't have to do for much longer. I know every band has to earn their stripes. They set up their equipment and take it down, but it's exhausting after being at work all day.

We have it down to a science, though. Within fifteen minutes are instruments are in place. The wires are where they are supposed to be and we have a few minutes to kill. I run down to the bar and ask for a few bottles of water. This is a bartender I don't know well, and Eric is down at the other side of the bar. "Can you open a tab and I'll take care of it after the show."

"Sure thing." He presses a few buttons on the computer and hands me the water.

I rush back to the stage and toss a water to both of my friends. Setting mine on the stool next to the microphone. I clear my throat and lean forward. "Hey Asheville, how are y'all doing tonight?"

* * *

"Y'all were great tonight." Lisa throws her arms around my neck before I've even made it down the stage stairs. My hand grips the railing to keep me from falling backward.

"Glad you made it in time." Now that we're off the stairs, my hands wrap around her waist and I pull her toward me. "It felt like the crowd really enjoyed the performance."

"I don't think I've seen that many people out on the floor since New Year's." Lisa voice is loud against my ear to be heard over the chatter of the bar.

It's nice she notices things like that, especially because I don't. Does that make me a bad performer? I don't think so. The entire time I'm on the stage, I'm doing what I can to keep the crowd engaged. Everything is based on vibes. The more energy the audience is putting out, the better we play. The intensity increases and it feels like we're untouchable.

Releasing my hold on her, I reach for her hand. "Let's grab a drink before they make last call."

"That should be in about five minutes." She glances at a clock on the wall. "It's one of the things I've learned in the class I'm taking."

I weave us through people on the way to the bar. "How are you liking class? Is it everything you thought it would be?"

Even though we've talked and messaged each other, we haven't talked much about music or bartending. There's too much stuff each of us missed during our time apart, and we spend that time filling each other in. We're getting reintroduced to one another.

"Well, there's this one guy in class who is a complete ass and rude for zero reason. But I've made a friend. Her name is Joan. She's a bit older than me and has two kids, but she wants to earn extra money on the weekends."

We squeeze into an open space at the bar, and Eric nods toward us. He finishes up his current order and starts on our drinks. At least, I think they're ours. I'm also not sure how I should feel about the fact she hasn't shared any of this with me prior to now. I've also never asked.

"That's awesome. How is the actual class?"

"Meh," she shrugs. "The instructor is kind of a hard ass, but he's good. I keep screwing up the drinks, though, and it's frustrating."

"Is he putting that pressure on you?" I've never understood teachers who do that because all it does is make the student, in whatever area, nervous. I dealt with it a lot in school when I was trying to keep some of my grades up to play football.

"No." She shakes her head and sighs. "It's all me. I have this need to be perfect in everything I do. Letting people down isn't an option."

Interesting. Even though I thought we knew each other well, I'm still learning things about her. My hope is it never stops. "We can always practice some things you've learned this weekend. We're both off on Sunday."

"That would actually be great." She claps her hands. "I'll run to a store tomorrow after my class and get some of the things we'll need. At least the basics."

Eric slides our drinks in front of us, and it's so weird seeing her drink martinis. It feels upscale and not at all like the person she used to be. Her tastes have changed, and I hope like hell I don't turn out to be something else she outgrows.

"Do you know how to make that?"

She nods before taking a sip. "Yeah, but mine doesn't turn out all that great. I'm working on it."

"That's all you can do. Wanna grab food after this?" I lift my mug of beer to explain what I mean.

"Yes. I'm starving." She looks behind us at my friends. "Are they coming?"

"Hell no." I wrap my arm around her shoulder. "They've

had me most of the week, and I haven't got to see you. It's just you and me tonight."

Twenty-four hour breakfast places used to be the best thing ever. Maybe it's because I was slightly inebriated when I used to go. Tonight...that was a bust. They couldn't get anything right, and it was packed. I did recognize a few people from the bar, so it's likely they had the same idea.

Lisa is following behind me as we pull into the driveway. I asked if she'd rather go home, but she was tired of Eric quizzing her every five minutes about the things she's learning in class.

She parks next to me and waits until I'm at the front door before she gets out of the car. I don't blame her. It's cold and windy. I wouldn't want to wait in it either.

"Thank you for brinner." She bumps into me as I unlock the door.

"Brinner?"

"Breakfast slash dinner. It's the easiest way to say it." She grins and walks inside as soon as I have the door open.

"If you say so." I follow and close the door behind me. Pulling my arms out of the sleeves of my jacket, I toss it on the bed. "Do you want to watch TV or something?"

"I'm good with something." She's half sitting on the table, half standing. Her arms behind her, bracing her body. Playful Lisa is probably my favorite version of her. She throws caution to the wind and goes with the flow.

Two steps. That's all I need in this small house to reach her. I settle between her legs and place my hands on her thighs. "Oh yeah? What kind of something?"

She cups my face in her hands and pulls me toward her. Her lips meet mine at the same time her legs circle my waist. I have to lift her and push her further onto the table to keep either of us from falling.

I lean forward, one hand braced on the table and the other circling her waist. There's a perfectly good bed five feet away, but I don't want to break this kiss.

She moves her hands down my body until reaching my jeans. Within seconds my jeans are unbuttoned and she's working on hers. Her legs coming down to rest against mine. She reaches up with one hand to hold herself steady and uses the other to push down her jeans. Lucky for her I have great balance, otherwise both of us would be on the floor.

This feels like old times. Not only the sex, but the spontaneity. We spent so many nights wrapped in each other arms for hours, only for her to lie on the bed and listen to me play guitar afterward. It's the first time I've felt like us since we got back together.

"Do you want to move to the bed?" I know what her answer is going to be, but I have to ask.

She nods, and I pick her up before carrying her to the bed. Her arms around my neck, holding tight, while I try not to trip over my falling jeans. Her fingers trail along my chest after I set her down and wrestle the fabric on my legs. I try to step out of my boots and pants at the same time and almost fall onto her.

"Slow down. We have all night."

"You don't have to be up early for anything?"

"Crap. No, I do. I have class at nine." She pulls me toward her again. "But it's okay. I can take a nap before I have to go into work."

"Are you sure?" Geez. I can't seem to keep my mouth shut. Why am I trying to put the brakes on this?

She nods her head, "yes. Now kiss me."

I've always been one to do what I'm told and my mouth crashes into hers. The wind is picking up, and the branches scratch against the house. It only adds to the intensity of being with her right now. My hands trail up and down her body, relishing every touch.

It's been almost a week since we've held each other and I'm not going to let tonight pass us by.

17
lisa

THE PAST WEEK has been brutal. Not because of the grueling schedule of working all day then heading off to class for four hours. No, it's because I haven't been able to spend any time with Devin.

He was still sleeping when I woke up this morning and I tiptoed out of his house before going to mine to get ready for class. Each time I talk to him on the phone, or to his face, there's a gnawing sense in my stomach that it will be the last. That we're on borrowed time. Once Crooked Halo scoops him up to go on tour with them, I know my time will be up.

Music is his life, and there's no way I can compete with that. I can't go on the road with him either. Not after Carlos and Angie paid for me to take this class and work the bar. I can't. No, I *won't*, do that to them.

"Ma'am?" The person at the counter says. Now I'm not sure how I feel about being called that. Surely, I'm not old enough to be a ma'am.

"Sorry, yeah?"

"Your total is \$105.23, and I need to see your ID." Thank God yesterday was payday. This is the only time I have to get the liquor to practice making drinks, and I only stuck to vodka and whiskey since that's what most people order. Or, that's what I assume based on the amount of bottles Carlos constantly has on order. Also, how is he going to ask for my license after calling me ma'am?

"Thanks." I pull out both cards and hand over the ID. He brings it close to his face as if I might be lying about my age. Finally, he types my birth date into the computer and hands the rectangular piece of plastic back to me. I insert my card into the machine and wait for it to approve before pulling it out.

It's only now that I realize I rarely come into liquor stores. Anytime I've wanted a drink, I've gone to a bar, usually one I'm working at. I grab the brown bag with the bottles and walk out.

Hopefully the bar isn't crazy tonight. Staying at Devin's last night wasn't the best idea, but I don't regret it. I needed to see him and spend time with him. He seemed to have needed it as well.

I have my doubts, though. It seems like more people were there to see Devin and his band than the last time. They are gaining popularity, and I wonder how long it will take for the high of being in the spotlight to overshadow our relationship. When will I become second choice?

Now isn't the time to worry about that, I get in my car and head home. A nap is needed if I'm going to make it until closing time tonight. Especially since Carlos wants me behind the bar again to observe. The only difference is this time I actually know a little bit about what's going on.

* * *

"No." Eric pulls the whiskey out of my hand. "That's too much."

I swear I'm going to murder my roommate before the end of the day. The bar is slow until the evening crowd picks up, and we're working on some of the drinks I've learned. Apparently, I suck at this.

"Too much what?" I can't seem to get the measurement right.

"All of it." He throws his hands up in exasperation.

"Then let me use the measuring cups until I get the hang of it." Carlos is letting use the cheap stuff to practice, and I feel bad about how much I've already wasted. "I'm just starting out."

"Measuring cups take too long when we're busy." He takes a deep breath and comes moves beside me, placing a hand on my shoulder. "You'll get the hang of it. Before long pouring drinks will feel natural."

It's a good thing he isn't my instructor for class. There's no way any of us would make it learning from him. "If you say so. Right now, I'm having doubts I'm cut out for this."

Eric moves the glass with my fourth failed whiskey sour attempt to the side and turns me toward him. "Carlos and Angie wouldn't go through all this trouble if they didn't think you could do it. It's not an easy job to learn, especially if you don't already have some knowledge about how everything works behind the bar."

"But I feel like no matter what I do I'm going to fail." There's nothing he can say that's going to convince me otherwise. Unless, of course, I magically become better at making drinks. I know it will take practice, but it feels unattainable right now.

"I promise, you'll learn and be amazing." He really is a good friend to have in my corner.

"Hey, whatcha got going on back there?" I've been so focused on complaining to Eric about my lack of skills, I didn't see my boyfriend come up to the bar.

"Making crappy drinks," I deadpan. "Why are you here so early? Y'all don't go on stage for a few more hours."

"I wanted to come get a drink and see you." Devin grins and it makes my heart melt. He's always so considerate, and I feel like I have one foot out the door before anything has even happened. "I know you're working, but I couldn't help myself. Aside from tomorrow, we won't see each other until the show in front of you know who."

The last sentence is a whisper. It's not public knowledge and he doesn't want anyone to overhear. "Let Eric know what you want. I'll screw it up."

"It can't be that bad."

"Wanna bet?" I pick up the whiskey sour Eric was losing his shit about, and set it on the counter in front of him. "This is the drink I made moments ago. Taste it, then tell me with a straight face it isn't awful."

Something over my shoulder catches his attention and he looks confused. Looking over my shoulder I see Eric doing hand motions, and when he notices me, he puts his hands down to his side. He doesn't have to tell everyone my business. I mean I know it's not everyone, but I value Devin's opinion more than anyone else.

"Before I drink it, tell me what it is. I usually stick to beer and want to know what I'm getting into."

"It's a whiskey sour." I slide the drink closer to him. He's going to regret this.

He places his hand around the short glass, and picks it up. Before he moves it to his lips, he waves it in a cheers motion. Pulling it to his mouth, he tips it up, and takes a big drink. It's a sipping drink, not something you shoot down as fast as you can. But I watch his face closely.

He swallows and does his best to hide his grimace. But I know the truth. "It's," he swallows again. "Not bad."

"You're lying." He's doing a bad job of it, too. "It's terrible."

"Really, Lisa." Devin sets the drink back on the counter. "I'm not saying it's the best thing I've ever drank, but it's not as bad as you make it out to be."

"Have you ever had a whiskey sour before? I can tell you that isn't what it tastes like." Eric was right, there's too much whiskey and simple syrup. The ratios aren't correct and this is way more than we should be serving.

"No." He finally relents. "Whiskey has never really been my thing."

"Eric, can you make him one so he knows what it's supposed to taste like."

"Are you sure you want me to do that?" I know he's trying his best to make me feel better about my horrible drink.

"Yep."

I turn to leave. There are other things that need to be done, and sitting here focusing on my failures isn't what I have in store for the day. Devin sets his hand on top of mine. A silent motion for me to stay.

"You'll get the hang of it. We'll practice tomorrow.: His gives my hand a light squeeze.

"Okay." I slide my hand from under his, and get back to work.

I watch him and Eric interact while I'm wiping down the bar. They seem to be getting along, and no longer trying to bite each other's heads off. Some of the stress in my body releases. I need for the two of them to get along. Eric is my roommate and will be around as long as I'm living there, and it's important that the two of them are on good terms.

"I'm taking my break," Eric calls over his shoulder as walks from behind the bar. "It won't be long, and the rush hasn't started yet."

"I hope it stays that way."

He waves off my concern and heads toward the office. After a few minutes, Devin leaves the bar as well. I have a feeling they are up to something, but I can't exactly leave to figure out what it is. There's another bartender here, at the other end of the bar, and I hope they know they get to pour all the drinks. Right now, the only thing I feel qualified to do is fill beer mugs. Anything other than that and I'm liable to screw it up.

The sky is darkening the closer it gets to night, and I know soon we'll have more customers than I can handle. I hope like hell Eric hurries back. He has this down to a science, and I won't be the one who screws up everything.

He finally makes it back, even though it's only been about ten minutes, and just in time. Large groups of people are coming through the door. Some of them bypass the stand and find a stool at the bar. I have a feeling it's going to be a very long night.

* * *

I didn't get home from the bar until the early hours of the morning. The crowd last night was a more rambunctious than usual, and it took us longer to clean up. It's growing pains since live music is something we do now. It'll get better and easier to manage once we have the kinks worked out.

Most people would still be sleeping, not me, though. I plan on perfecting that damn whiskey sour if my life depends on it. Then I'll practice drinks with vodka before moving on to margaritas. Those I know how to make, but I want to fine tune it.

There's a knock at the door. There's only one person it could be, and I'm shocked he's here since they played right up until closing time. If it were me, I'd still be passed out in bed.

He's an early bird, though, and it's something I'll never understand.

Rounding the kitchen counter, I make my way to the door. I check over my body, but I look like a mess. I'm still in my jammies, and my hair is thrown in a bun with pieces of hair sticking out all over the place. It's not cute. It's the best he's going to get, though...for now. If we go somewhere later on today, I'll actually get ready to be seen in public.

I open the door and his hand is raised mid-knock. "You're up early."

"So are you. I wasn't sure if you'd be awake." He has a closed box in his other hand, and I want to know what's in it. "Can I come in?"

"Oh, yeah, sure." I open the door wider, and he steps inside. "You could have called to make sure I was awake."

"True, but then I wouldn't have been able to surprise you with my visit."

"It's not really a surprise since you were supposed to come over anyway." We had this planned since we won't be able to see each other until his show on Friday when that band will be here to scope out new acts.

"You've got me there." He closes the door behind him as I rush to the living room to turn down the music on the TV. He sets the box on the counter next to the open liquor bottles. I probably should have invited more people over today so they can taste test, but right now I'm only trying to get the measurements right since that's what I have the hardest time with. Devin looks around the room. "Where's Eric? I didn't see his car in the driveway."

I toss the remote on the sofa, soft sounds of alternative rock fill the room. "He'll be back later. Apparently, he goes to see his mom on Sundays and comes back with a ton of food." Shrugging my shoulders I make me way over to the kitchen, ignoring the pang in my heart that I don't have a mom I even want to see after the way she left me to my own devices as a kid. "What's in the box?"

"Oh." He opens it up and pulls out a small box. "Donuts." He hands them to me and I waste no time digging in. "And the rest is different cups and measuring things Eric gave me last night."

"For what?"

"To help you with making drinks." At me confused stare, he adds, "he said it's too hard to teach you at the bar when you have customers. So, he gave me these when he went on break so you could use them to practice."

"He could have given them to me himself." Especially after his comments yesterday.

"I know, but he thought you'd be less frustrated taking them from me." He's not wrong. "Want to work on your first drinks?"

This is why I fell for this man in the first place, and why I'm pretty sure I love him. Despite all my fears surrounding his music and what that means for us, he truly is my biggest supporter.

"Sure, but be prepared to order in food because I think by the time we've taste tested them, we'll be buzzed."

"I can get down with that." He grins and wraps an arm around my waste before kissing me on the temple. As much as I'd rather curl into bed with him. I know I need to get this down. "What's first?"

18
devin

EVEN THOUGH LISA and I have just gotten back together, I can feel her pulling away. It could be because we're both stressed, but I don't think it's the main cause of it. She seemed so happy to be back together until I mentioned Crooked Halo coming to scope out talent. Since then, conversations about my band and what we hope to accomplish have be stilted.

It's odd because before that she was one of my biggest supporters with my music aside from my parents. She wanted to hear everything and look over my lyrics. Now she doesn't even ask. I have to bring it up.

It may be the middle of the week, but I'm off work today. Rain tends to delay construction work, and it's coming down too heavily for us to do anything. Normally, I'd stay home and let the dreary mood inspire words, but I can't today. I need to see Lisa before she goes to work.

Her favorite donuts are sitting in the seat next to me. Coffee is in the cupholder, and I hope like hell she's actually awake.

Pulling up to the curb in front of her house, I take a few

moments to gather my thoughts. A part of me wonders if I should bring up what's on my mind with her. Things could go one of two ways. She'll open up, or she'll skip town again. The last one is unlikely, but after last time it's something I can't discount.

Rain drops hit the windshield in rapid succession. The sky is full of dark, ominous clouds. The perfect weather for cuddling. Or, blowing up all the progress Lisa and I have made. It could go either way.

Turning off the truck, I gather the donuts and coffee in my hands. Hopefully I don't drop either. With the rain coming down, it's not a time to dawdle. I open the door, and climb out of the truck, shutting the door with my foot before running up the walkway to the porch.

I don't have time to adjust the items and knock because the door is already opening in front of me. Instead of Lisa on the other side, it's Eric. "Ah, how nice you brought me coffee?"

"You wish." I roll my eyes and walk inside. "Where's Lisa?"

"Her room." He closes the door. "I think she's awake, but I'm not sure. I've learned not to mess with her in the mornings."

"She can be grumpy that's for sure."

"Which is weird because outside of that she's happy as can be." Eric shrugs his shoulders as if that small motion explains Lisa's feelings toward mornings. "Good luck if she's not awake."

"Thanks." I make my way down the hall. In just a few short weeks, I've gotten over any insecurities I had about Eric being her roommate. He's proven time and again, he only wants to be her friend. I also know Lisa would never give him a chance in hell. He's not her type.

I knock lightly on the door, but don't get a response. Turning the knob, I enter slowly, doing my best not to wake her if she's still asleep. To my surprise she's sitting up in her bed, a book opened on her lap and a pen in her hand.

"Good morning." Since she didn't respond to the knock, I'm hoping my voice will pull her out of her thoughts. But there's nothing.

My steps are slow as I walk toward her bed. I don't want to scare her. Setting the donuts and coffee on the table beside her bed. Whatever she's doing, she's completely focused because she still hasn't noticed my presence.

I climb onto the bed beside her and she finally realizes she isn't alone. Her eyes meet mine and widen. She pulls her earbuds out, and faint music can be heard playing through them. That explains why she couldn't hear me. "When did you get here?"

"A few minutes ago." I reach over to the table and grab the box and cup. "I brought you breakfast."

"Thanks." She takes my offering and opens the donuts. "Why aren't you at work?"

I point toward the window. "It's raining, and we can't do anything."

"That makes sense." She takes a bite of her donut and refocuses on the book in front of her.

"What are you doing?" I tap the book. It looks like a bunch of recipes.

"Studying." She moves the book off her lap and sets in front her. "We have to show that we know how to make drinks the next couple of nights as a sort of test before we get our certification."

"You'll do great." I bump into her, doing anything I can to lessen the tension radiating off her. "Even Eric agreed the drinks you made Sunday were good."

"I know, and I feel more confident with the different types of drinks, but making those, I wasn't under any sort of pressure." She sighs and leans into me. "There weren't customers waiting on me to get them drinks as quickly as possible. That's what has me concerned. And then you have your big performance this weekend and I feel like I'm spinning in too many different directions."

Now I know for sure my music is part of the reason she's having a hard time. Though, I'm not sure why. "What does my performance have to do with anything?"

"Nothing really." She won't look at me and I know it's a lie. If it was nothing, she wouldn't have brought it up and it wouldn't be adding to her stress.

"It's obviously not nothing." I need to get to the bottom of this. Need to know she's in my corner regardless of what happens. Because right now, it feels like she doesn't give a damn and it hurts. It's a big part of my life and something I want to pursue outside of playing on the small stage here in Asheville. If she's not on board with that I need to know.

She buries her face in her hands and takes a few deep breaths. For a second, I don't think she's going to say anything. The room is silent and it adds to the building pressure. Finally, she moves her hands. Leaning back, she focuses on the ceiling, doing everything in her power not to make eye contact with me.

"I know music is your life, and you want to do big things with it, but that scares me. I just got back to town, and we're building something new. When Crooked Halo picks you to go on tour with them, where does that leave us?" She doesn't say it but what she really wants to know is where it leaves her.

"That's not going to happen. Me and you," I point between us even though she can't see me. "We'll figure out how to make it work. That's what couples do. Nothing is going to change between us. And you're assuming my band getting picked is inevitable."

She throws the comforter off of her, the box of donuts knocked over, and climbs out of bed. I pick the food up and put it back in in the box as I watch her pace back and forth in front of her dresser. She seems to be gathering her thoughts, and I don't know what to do to help.

"There's no way they aren't going to pick your band. Y'all are that good. Which means everything will change. You'll be on the road touring, and I'll be here bartending and wondering when I'm going to see you next."

"That's not about to happen. I don't know what I can do or say to show you I'm nothing like her." I get off her bed and face her. "I'm not your mom. There's no way in hell I can forget that you exist."

The minute the words are out of my mouth, I know I've made a huge mistake. Lisa looks as if I just slapped her even though I'm on the opposite side of the room. Deep down I know all of this stems from her abandonment issues, and fear of loneliness. I don't know how I can prove I won't be the cause of that. And, honestly, it shouldn't fall on me to do all the work when she already is halfway out the door.

Lisa takes a few moments to school her features, and wipe all the emotion from her face. "I think you should leave."

"Look, I'm sorry." I take a few steps around the bed in her direction, but she holds up her hands, warding me away. "I shouldn't have said that. We should talk about it."

"Not right now, Devin." She runs her hands through her hair, her fingers getting caught in tangles. "I'll see you at your show this weekend."

There's no room for argument. A part of me wants to at least hug her bye, but I know that won't help matters. She did say she's coming to the show, so I'm hopeful it means this isn't the end for us. That she's only temporarily putting up walls and she'll think things through. Then we can talk about it and figure us out.

Instead of approaching her, I turn to her bedroom door. "Will you at least let me know when you make it home from class tonight? The storms aren't supposed to end until tomorrow."

"I will."

Opening it and walking out, I can't help but wonder how I fucked things up so badly. Besides the part where I told her I wasn't her mom. That was a shitty thing for me to do, and I do regret it.

Eric is sitting on the couch, watching a news show when I walk out. "Is everything okay?"

"Not really," I walk straight to the front door, "just letting you know she's not in a good mood, so tread carefully." I hope he realizes now isn't the time to go in there and be a mother hen. She'll talk when she's ready. I only hope that's sooner rather than later.

"Thanks for the warning." He stands, approaches me and shakes my hand. "Be careful out there, man. The weather guy said there could be tornados."

"I'll keep my eye on the news." It's not like I'll be out on the roads. There's only one place calling to me. The weather just happens to match my emotions. Fear and possible turmoil. Without another word I walk out.

* * *

I stopped at my house long enough to grab my notebook and pen. One of the days I'll remember to keep one of each in my truck. My clothes are soaked from getting in and out of the truck. It could have been avoided if had what I needed on me. But there are other songs I want to work on that are written inside this shabby notebook.

The garage door is closed. The rain beating against the metal and trees scraping against the outside of the building. I rummage through the small box in the back of the room for any extra clothes I may have hidden away in here. I need to get out of these clothes. It may match my mood, but it's uncomfortable. Finally, I find a pair of sweats and a t-shirt. I make quick work of getting changed and toss my clothes in a pile on the floor.

The rain seems to be getting louder, as well as the thunder. I hope like hell Lisa is careful when she drives to class later. If she was actually speaking to me right now, I'd probably drive her myself. But that's not the case because I can't keep my big mouth shut. I should have left it to her to tell me what was wrong in her own time.

I grab a soda out of the fridge and plop on the old couch. My pen bouncing off the notebook and onto the floor. Can nothing go right today? Bending over, I pick it up from the floor before leaning back. I grab the notebook and flip through the pages, looking for songs that need some editing. But words about my failures kept bouncing around in my head and I find the first empty page.

The pen flies across the page. The words flowing more than they have since that first night Lisa stayed over. This song doesn't have the same vibe, though. It's sadness, fear, and a hope at redemption for both of us. Everything I wish I would have said to Lisa in her room is filling the page of this notebook. Not all of it is usable, but some of it will be. If we get our ass in gear with practice, we may be able to perform it this weekend.

Is it a good idea? Probably not. But I'm laying everything out on the table. It'll be up to Lisa to decide if she wants to continue where we've seemed to leave off. To give us a real chance without fear overwhelming her.

The side door bangs against the wall as it opens. I bolt upright and rush to close it, thinking the wind blew it open, but Trey and Cash are running inside to get out of the storm.

"What are y'all doing here?" What time is it for that matter? I haven't looked at my phone since I started writing. I pick it up off the couch and look at the time. Holy shit. It's been *hours*.

"Are we not having practice today?" Trey looks around the room. "I figured because we have the big showdown this weekend, you'd want us here as early as possible."

"Sorry, I was in my own little world. I'm good to practice now." I turn back toward the couch. "Actually, I wanted to run this new song by you."

"When did you write it?" Cash asks as he takes the notebook.

"It's what I've been working on all day."

Cash reads over it for a few minutes. "It's deep, man." He pauses for a second and taps his foot. "But I think I know a beat that will work well with it. Do you want to perform it this weekend?"

"If we can pull it off, but I don't want to play something that isn't ready."

"For sure." He hands the notebook over to Trey. "I'm thinking slow and soulful, what about you?"

Trey reads it over nodding as his eyes pass over each line. "Let's do this."

Both of them go toward their instruments, ready to see what we can make of this new song. I have a feeling this will be the one that gets Crooked Halo's attention.

19
lisa

I **FEEL** like an asshole for blowing up at Devin the way I did the other day. Eric hasn't made things any better either. He wants my whole life story so he can *help* me work through it. I don't want help through it. I just need people to understand I have my own scars from the past. It's hard to let go of them.

Today is the last day of testing. Tomorrow, we get our certification and I'm done with coming to this class. The only plus side is our instructor moved classes to earlier in the day because he had something come up tonight. I should get back to Asheville in time for Devin and his friends to go on stage, assuming traffic isn't a nightmare.

"Hey, you okay?" Joan whispers to me as the class douche fails to make the drink he's been given. It fills me with a tiny bit of satisfaction to know he's struggling as bad as me. The only difference is I've been studying. On breaks, before work, and sometimes even when I get home from class. I've been taking it seriously to be the best I can be.

"Yeah, just nervous." I hope like hell she doesn't press me anymore, even though I have a feeling she'll ask again later.

"You're going to do great." She points toward the guy

everyone can't stand, and laughs. "I mean we all have to do better than him, right? Look how much liquor he's wasting on the bar."

"You're right." I can't help the giggle that bubbles up. If there's one thing about this class I love, it's the friendship I've formed with Joan. I'm going to miss her when this is over. Or, maybe I can talk to Angie and Carlos. She said she only wants to work on the weekends and that's when we're busiest. Plus, she'll have Sundays off. It's a win-win.

"I think I'm up next." She fidgets with her fingers and I wonder if she's come up with a way to memorize the basic drinks. He did say we weren't going to do anything fancy.

"You've got this." She walks up to the bar with confidence and goes over the setup procedure. The instructor asks a few questions and she answers them without an issue. He has her make a margarita, and I can see the relief she feels at the choice. It's simple and something she already knew how to make. It's not long before she's standing beside me once again. "I told you." I bump my shoulder into hers.

"Thank God he chose margaritas. Otherwise, I would be screwed. There are very few drinks I can make off the top of my head, and I know I'll need a cheat sheet taped to whatever bar I work at until I get it down."

"Don't worry about it. I'm sure you'll pick it up in no time."

My name is called next, and my feet feel like they are glued to the floor. I can do this. He calls my name again and Joan gives me a little nudge forward. She's such a good friend. It's the push I need to move my feet forward.

The bar set up is similar to Out of the Ashes. I think that's what makes it easier when I'm watching behind the bar. I finish doing the setup process and wait for my instructions, a smile on my face because I know that brings in great tips.

The instructor waits a few moments, leaving me in

suspense. It's question time, and I am completely ready for this part. First, he asks me what date people have to have been born in order to be served. That's easy. Then he asks me what the serving limit is for patrons. It takes me a few moments to answer that one. But when I do, he nods.

I glance at the liquor bottles left. So far margarita and whiskey are gone. There's a bottle of vodka, gin, rum, and brandy. Now I'm anxious over what drink he's going to have me make. There's only three I practiced with and two of them are out.

He crooks his head to the side, no doubt trying to decide which drink to give me. I do my best to exude confidence. My back and shoulders are straight. I don't fidget, or make any move that can be construed as nerves. "Lisa, I'd like you to make a martini."

Okay, there are a few ways to make this, and I need to clarify even though I feel like the question is straight out of that action move. "Sir, shaken or stirred?"

He smiles and nods appreciatively. It appears I've passed that little test. And this is another one I've practiced. I grab the vermouth and vodka. He doesn't take off points if we use a measuring cup so I grab the stainless-steel cup that looks like an hour glass. Flipping it over until the correct measurement is facing up, I add the vodka until it hits the line. I grab the scoop and pour ice into the shaker before adding the vodka and splash of vermouth. Putting the top on the shaker I give it a few good shakes. One thing I learned is I need two hands to do the shaker. Those people who use one are freaking rock-stars and I hope to be like them one day.

Setting the shaker down, I grab the martini glass and add vermouth to it before swirling it around and dumping it. Next is pouring the vodka mixture in. I grab a toothpick and two olives to finish off the drink and slide it across the bar top.

It felt like I was doing the motions in slow motion and like it was taking forever, but honestly, it's been a couple of minutes max. He reaches out and takes a sip. "It's good, Lisa. Where did you learn the vermouth trick in the glass?"

"A friend of mine when I was practicing make the drinks at home."

He nods appreciatively. "Keep them around. They know what they're doing." As if I'd ever let Eric stop being my friend. He's annoying as hell sometimes, but he's always looks out for me. Even if it comes with some tough love.

I make my way back over to the line of students waiting for their turn. Joan wraps me in a hug. "You did amazing. It's a good thing you have a job lined up after this."

"You know I could always hook you up with a job."

"Really?"

"Absolutely. I know my bosses are always looking for good help."

"Thank you so much." The both of us step back from the group, letting them discuss amongst themselves. "So, when are you going to spill the beans about what is really going on with you? I know it wasn't just over the test."

For someone who has known me for a short amount of time, she sure does get me. I wonder if it's something that comes with age. I mean she's not a lot older than me, but she seems to have some wisdom I can desperately use. Things I can't go to Delilah about because Devin is her brother.

"So, the guy I've been seeing, he's in a band. There's a popular band who is coming to the bar tonight to see them and a few other bands play. They'll be there tomorrow night, too. The whole reason they are coming is because they want to bring someone on tour with them. And I have a feeling my boyfriend's band will be picked."

Gah, saying it like that sounds dumb and selfish on my part. But it's something I can't get over. The constant need to make sure people in my life aren't going to leave me behind.

Even though that's exactly what I did when I left Asheville the first time, and what I've done for most of my adult life. I run. Plus, the fact that I couldn't even say he's my boyfriend because I'm not sure that's true anymore. We haven't talked since I told him to leave aside from a few texts making sure I got home okay.

"Are there some underlying issues there? Because I'd think you'd be excited for him. That sounds like a pretty big deal."

I tell her everything I went through as kid. The way my mom would forget I even existed, and when she did remember how badly she treated me. How she'd leave me alone for days at a time and I'd have to figure out how to feed myself. My only saving grace was we had neighbors who paid attention and would bring me food when they noticed my mom leave. All she cared about was men and material things. I was the thing that got in the way of that.

"Look, honey, you can tell me if I'm overstepping, but I think you should see a therapist."

"What? I don't need one of those." Do I?

"I'm not saying you do." She places a hand on her shoulder, reassuring me. "But it might be a good idea to talk to one and work past the trauma of your childhood. Because that's what it is...trauma. And it affects every other relationship you have in your life until you start to work through it."

I never really thought of it that way. I know I had a shitty childhood, but so many other kids had it way worse than I ever did. "Do you really think it could help?"

"Yes, I do. You can't live your life in fear of everyone treating you the same way, and if you find the right one, they will help you come to terms with that."

She's right. I do live my life in fear. Fear of disappointing people. Of people leaving me behind. Not being enough. It's the reason I run so much, until Asheville. There was no point in getting close to people. Then...they couldn't hurt me. I've done one thing that scares me today. Maybe it's time to do something else.

There are two more people who need to go though and make a drink, then class will be dismissed and I can head back to Asheville. I'm not sure I can do it alone, though. "Hey Joan, what plans do you have tonight?"

"Nothing really," she shrugs, "my dad and step-mom have the kids until tomorrow after class. I was going to go home and have a self-care night."

"What do you think about going to see some bands play tonight?"

She bites her lip. "I don't know. It's kind of far for me to drive down there and back by myself."

"Don't worry about that, you can stay at my place. I'm sure my roommate won't mind." I'm willing her to say yes with everything in me. I also can't help but wonder if she's been through something similar and that's why she suggested therapy. Maybe she does know how I feel.

She takes a few moments to think it over and nods. "Okay, I'll go see your boyfriend play tonight."

"Let's hope he's still my boyfriend." I wrap my arms around her shoulders and give her a hug. "Do you want to follow me or ride with me?"

"I'll follow that way I can leave early to get ready before class."

"Sounds like a plan." Both of us return to our classmates, watching the last person make their drink. My phone vibrates in my pocket and I pull it out to see who it is.

ERIC

I think they might get started earlier than they planned.

LISA

Okay. We're almost done here and I'll be on my way.

ERIC

I was wrong about him. And whatever happened y'all need to fix it. He looks miserable.

LISA

That's the plan.

I feel horrible that I've made him feel that way. Eric could be exaggerating, but I doubt he is. Especially if Devin feels the same way I do. These past couple of days have been brutal. As much as I've wanted to stay home and wallow in my self-pity, I couldn't. Now, I'm glad I didn't. There's a plan forming in my head, and I fully intend on carrying it out.

My phone dings again.

DELILAH

You're coming to see Devin play tonight, right?

LISA

Yes. I'm leaving soon.

DELILAH

Hurry. Apparently, someone leaked that CH is here tonight, and the parking lot is filling up.

LISA

Crap. Okay just make sure there's enough room in the bar for two people to come in.

DELILAH

Who are you bringing? And I hope you know whatever happens between you and my brother, I'm still your friend.

Damn, did we send out a memo about having problems? I haven't talked to anyone, and I don't think he has. But we have an awesome circle of friends who know us better than we know ourselves. I purposefully didn't talk to Del because he's her brother and I won't put her in the middle out of respect.

LISA

It's the girl I befriended in class. And that
means a lot. See you soon.

I put my phone back in my pocket. The last person is done making their drink. Despite the minor problems with some of my classmates, I think we all did a decent job. Even the douchebag. We break down the bar and clean everything up.

Joan follows me out the door. "In case we lose each other in traffic, here's the address. You are going to love our bar."

"I'll see you there." She waves and climbs into her car.

Climbing into mine, I waste no time pulling out of the parking lot. I have a relationship to fix and then I need to do as Joan suggested and try to fix myself.

20
devin

"ARE YOU READY TO HEAD OUT?" Cash pats me on the shoulder. "We should probably get there early enough to see the other band."

We're sitting in my garage drinking water. Honestly, I need something stronger, but I don't want to drink and drive. Plus, there's the added embarrassment of looking like fools in front of the very people we're trying to impress.

"Yeah, let's head that way." We aren't doing anything here except freaking ourselves out. It'll do us no good. At least if we're at the bar, we'll be surrounded by people who support us. Folks who keep coming back week after week to watch us do our thing.

"We riding together, or taking separate cars?" Trey asks as he grabs his bottle of water. "I don't care either way."

"All the equipment is in the truck, right?" Even if Crooked Halo doesn't pick us, I think we need to invest in a trailer.

"Yep." Trey nods and heads toward the door.

"Then we can all ride together." I stand and join my friends by the door. We still don't have a name, and we'll need to fix that soon. Right now, all that matters is we go on the stage and perform to the best of our ability while having fun doing it.

"Are you sure?" Cases asks as we walk outside. It's already dark and I flip on the floodlight so we can see.

"Why wouldn't I be?"

"Because a certain lady friend will be there." Trey grins. "We don't want to get in the way of true love."

If only it were that. She would have talked to me by now if it was. I don't even know if she'll be there. She hasn't mentioned it since right before I left her house on Wednesday. There's a good chance she's getting packed up to leave after she finishes the bartending class.

"It's fine." They follow me to the truck. Trey gets in the backseat but Cash doesn't immediately climb in. "What's up?"

"Oh, nothing with me. I just wanted to reassure you she'll be there."

"You can't know that." Especially when I don't.

"Maybe not." He shrugs and rounds the front of the truck to the passenger side. "But I have a gut feeling that everything will be okay."

I'm glad he thinks so because right now I'm barely holding onto any hope that she wants to work things out.

* * *

The band playing before us is unloading and I park a few spaces away until they are done. We need to form a game plan. "Are we good to sing the new song tonight? Does it feel like we've gotten the kinks worked out?"

"Hell yeah," Trey slaps the back of my seat. "I think it should be the last song we play."

"Why not in the middle?" Cash turns in his seat until he can see our friend.

"Because it's new. And, it's an amazing song." He shakes his head and laughs. "You save the best for last. It's like you two don't know what you're doing sometimes."

"We'll go with your plan." He has a point. "We'll start with one of the crowd favorites, then play a few off our normal list, and end with the new one. Sound good to everyone?"

"Yep." Cash points out the front window. "It looks like they've finished unloading. Let's get our gear inside." I put the truck in gear and Cash asks, "Are we going first or last?"

"Last. One of the perks of being a regular band. We get special treatment." Not that we need it, but I want to see exactly what this other band is like.

The area behind the stage is clear and the other band is on the stage setting up. We place our instruments against the back wall before making our way to the bar area. I glance around the space to see if I can find the members of Crooked Halo.

My eyes bounce right over them before realizing they are here. They are settled around a table in the back corner. My guess is they are trying to stay unseen. If word gets out, they're here, this place is going to fill up...quick.

I keep moving so I don't tip anyone off. Eric is behind the bar and pouring drinks for a few people in the stools. When he sees me, he nods his head in acknowledgment. Within a few moments, he's coming toward the three of us with mugs. "Here you go."

"Man, we were trying to keep from drinking until after we perform." I try to push the drinks back.

"One beer isn't going to kill your vibe." He pushes the mug to me again. "I can tell you're nervous, this will help ease it."

"I'm only drinking it because you already made it."

"Smart man." He taps his knuckles on the bar and checks to make sure nobody is looking for another drink. "Have you talked to her?"

I shake my head and stare at the counter. If there's one thing I'm nervous about, it's her not showing up to support me. Not that I blame her. I was out of line. My only wish is she would have let me stay so we could talk it out. But she pushed me out...again.

"She'll come around. Just give her time. I haven't known her long, but she'll talk when she's ready."

"I know." Taking a drink of my beer, I do my best to keep my thoughts from going down a dark hole. It's not what I need to be focusing on right now. "I'll wait until she is. I can't let her slip away again."

"You're good people." Eric slaps the counter top. "I misjudged you in the beginning, but my roomie would be making a mistake if she didn't put in some effort." He notices someone come into the bar. "I need to get back to work. If you decide you want another drink, let me know. You can also come grab some water any time."

"Thanks." I lift my beer in salute. Turning toward the stage, I watch the band finish set up. They play a few notes on their instruments to check the sound and turn toward the side of the stage.

Leaning over, I see who they are looking at. Stella is giving them a thumbs up. This is the first night since New Years that I've seen her during live music nights. She probably wants to make sure everything goes off without a hitch. She had a hand in setting this up, and I have a feeling if all goes well, she'll look into doing battles here at some point.

The band has already started playing and I missed their name. Tonight, isn't the night to be in my head. We have a job to do, and hopefully we're picked by Crooked Halo.

This band is pretty good. A little heavier on the rock side, which makes sense. It's along the same lines of what Crooked Halo plays, but they haven't listened to us, yet. My fingers itch to get pick the guitar strings while we wait for them to finish.

The bar is filling up, and at first, I think it's the normal crowd. But with each passing minute, more and more people show up. It can only mean someone saw the members of Crooked in the back and spread the word.

In all honesty, I don't even care about that. I'm keeping a look out for the one person I want here most, and I still haven't seen her. There isn't much longer for the guys on stage to play and we'll have to begin our set up.

My beer is gone when I lift the mug to my lips, and I didn't realize I'd already emptied it. After setting it on the bar, I tap Trey and Cash. "Let's go back stage. But get some waters first."

We didn't even have to ask for them. Six water bottles are placed in front of us. Eric always has our backs when it comes to hydration and I can't believe I ever misjudged him. He's protective of those he considers friends. The folks who work here are lucky to have him looking out for them.

Now it's time to get my head focused. All that matter is getting on that stage and playing our hearts out. Hopefully Lisa will be here in time to witness it. Or, at least, hear the song I wrote about us, and for her.

* * *

The dance floor is full of people, and there isn't room for anyone to actually dance. The thick crowd makes it hard to search for Lisa, but I haven't seen her. I can't focus on that right now, though.

I strum a few notes on my guitar and the crowd claps. "Good evening, Asheville! How y'all doin' tonight?"

We're met with cheers, whoops, and clapping. For a few moments, I don't think they are going to stop, but finally they quiet down. "We're going to start off with one of your favorites. Sing along if you know it."

We begin playing our song about driving the backroads and dancing in empty fields with friends. It's a tribute to my high school years when we'd all gather at an empty field, playing music, drinking, and having the time of our lives. To my shock people are actually singing along.

A motion at the door catches my attention, Lisa moves until she's at the edge of the crowd. She made it. A weight lifts off my shoulder. It means she still cares. I don't miss a beat though.

We switch effortlessly to another song. People are still singing. It's surreal to hear. We haven't even performed that many times, and folks in the area know our music enough to belt the lyrics at the top of their lungs.

With each song Lisa moves closer to the stage. Pushing her way through the crowd to me.

It's almost time to play the last song, but I motion for the guys to keep playing a rhythm. "We have one more song for y'all, but I wanted to take a second to introduce my band mates. We don't have a name yet, and hope y'all can help us with that in the future. But on bass, we have Trey." The crowd goes wild for my goofy friend. "Cash is back there on drums." Another cheer for him. "And I'm Devin." The roar of the audience is deafening.

This is the life. Making music folks love and connecting with them. The people in this room right now are part of our journey no matter what happens with Crooked Halo.

"This is our last song for the night. It's a new one and I wrote it with a very important person in mind. She means everything to me, and we hope y'all enjoy it."

A collective "aw" rumbles through the crowd and I nod for Cash to count it out. The beat is slow, but powerful. The audience seems to understand this song will be emotional. People who came with a partner wrap their arms around each other and sway to the music.

I begin singing the story of me and Lisa. Our flirtatious beginning, how I thought I lost her forever only to have another chance with her. She's now directly in front of me. Her hands on the stage.

My voice belts out the promise to never hurt her and to always be there to comfort her when she needs it and be strong for her when she feels like she can't handle things. All of the promises I intend to keep wrapped into the lyrics of this song.

I look down until our eyes meet. Tears run down her face, but she's smiling and I know without a doubt we'll be okay. Everyone must sense the importance of this moment because not a word is uttered among them. Flashlights from their phones fill the darkness, and I hope Lisa knows how much she means to me.

The song winds down and I move the microphone to keep this moment between me and her. "I love you."

Apparently, I didn't move the mic far enough away because shouts of "kiss her" come from the crowd. Lisa looks for a way to get on the stage, but she's blocked on all sides. A few people around her offer up their hands, and they lift her to the stage.

She doesn't hesitate. Once she has her balance, her arms are around me and lips crash into mine. The entire building cheers, but I block them out. The only person that matters is the woman wrapped around me. She breaks the kiss and pulls back. "I love you, too."

The roar of the crowd comes back, and I bring the microphone to my mouth with Lisa held firmly to my side. "Thank y'all for an amazing night. We'll be back soon."

Cash hurries to cut the mic. None of us make a move to break down our set. Instead, Lisa pulls me down the stairs, through a throng of people, and down the hallway to the back office.

Once inside she closes the door behind us. "You were

amazing. I'm so sorry I let my own fears almost get in the way of us."

"It's okay." I run my fingers through her hair. "I knew deep down we would be end game."

"And you wrote a freaking song about us." She leans in and kisses me again. Not for long, but long enough that I don't want it to end. "If Crooked Halo doesn't pick y'all to tour with them, they will have missed an opportunity."

"How is that going to affect us, if they do? I won't do anything that jeopardizes our relationship."

"We'll figure it out. It's not fair of me to ask you not to chase your dreams. I'm done letting fear hold me back."

"Same." This time I pull her to me, my mouth is inches from hers when there's a knock on the door. "Should we get that?"

"Probably," she giggles. "It's not like this is my office or anything. It could be Stella."

She pulls away from me to open the door. It's not Stella on the other side. The members of Crooked Halo walk in, and I can't help but feel like this is going to be life changing.

"Devin, right?" The lead singer asks.

"Y-yeah," I stutter. I've never been one to get nervous in front of people, but this is different. They hold the fate of my future in their hands.

"Nice to meet you, I'm Dale." He holds his hand out to shake my hand, and my palms are too sweaty for this. I grip his hand and we shake briefly. "You did good out there, and you're our pick for tonight. You and whoever wins tomorrow night will tour with us."

"Seriously?"

"Yes." Dale laughs and hands me a card. "Get with your bandmates and we'll go over contracts and details."

"I will."

"Try to call me sooner than later." They turn to walk out

the door. "And we have to get to work on giving you a band name."

As soon as they leave the room, Lisa throws herself at me and I lift her off the ground, twirling her in a circle. "We did it."

"Yes, you did. And you deserve it."

"Wanna celebrate tonight?" I wink so she gets the meaning.

"Crap, I can't. I brought my friend Joan from bartending class, and she's crashing with me tonight because she didn't want to drive back," she winces, "sorry."

"It's all good. I almost forgot the guys rode with me."

"Tomorrow," she nods. "That's when we'll celebrate. Your new career and my certification. Expect an amazing present."

"I have no doubt." I kiss her long and deep before pulling away. "Shall we go tell our friends."

"Definitely." Lisa wraps her arm around my waist and we make our way out of the office.

Everything I've ever dreamed of has come true. I'll get to perform in front of crowds with my best friends, and I have the most amazing woman I've ever met by my side. What more could I ask for?

epilogue

IT'S BEEN three months since Devin and his friends signed the contract to go on tour with Crooked Halo. I won't lie and say it's been easy having him on the road, but it does make the time he's home more special.

He wanted me to go on the road with him, but the time away is good. My therapist is helping me heal from my childhood, and it makes my relationship with Devin healthier. He's even gone to a few sessions with me so he can see where I'm coming from, and I think it helps him understand me better.

I'm grabbing a bottle of whiskey from the shelf to make a martini for a customer. The bar is packed tonight. It's weird not hearing my boyfriend play while I'm working, but there is so much talent coming through the doors. We get to be a part of their story, and I feel pride in that.

"Hey," someone is calling from the other side of the bar, "can I get a whiskey sour?"

I turn and Devin is leaning against the bar, a huge smile splayed across his face. "Hey stranger, don't you usually drink beer?"

"What can I say?" he shrugs, "this beautiful bartender

made me try her godawful sample, then made me keep tasting them until they were perfect. It grew on me."

I glance at Joan and silently ask if she'll watch my end of the bar. She nods, and I take off. I round the opening to the bar until I'm standing in front of my boyfriend. "I didn't know you were going to be home this weekend."

"I wanted to surprise you." He pulls me onto his lap and kisses the side of my neck. "Did it work?"

"Definitely." I lean into him. Soaking up this tiny moment before I have to get back to work. "Do you really want a whiskey sour?"

"Of course. They've gotten way better since your first one."

"It's not nice to mock me." I swat at his shoulder as I stand up. "I'll get you one though. When do you leave again?"

"I'm home for a bit." I start toward the entrance to the bar, but he grabs my hand, pulling me to him again. "I was thinking. While I'm home, maybe we can look for a house."

That's a shocker. We've talked about it before, but nothing serious. "Do you think that's a good idea?"

"Yes," Eric calls from behind me. "I'm tired of having to look for a scrunchy on the door like I live in a damn dorm."

"Well, I guess the roomie has spoken," I laugh. "I'd love nothing more than move in with you."

People are making their way to the bar as the band on stage takes a break, and Devin notices. "I'll let you get back to work."

Within a minute I'm back behind the bar just in time to overhear Eric talking to Devin. "You have to put in a good word for me with Joan," he glances in her direction, "she's not falling for my usual flirting."

"That's because it sucks." I butt in. "She doesn't have time for your games."

"Nobody said I was playing games." He puts his hand to

his chest in mock offense. "I only want to get to know her outside of work."

"I'll see what I can do." Devin lowers his voice, but not enough. I can hear him. He'll do no such thing, but I'm not going to argue my case right now.

Making his drink doesn't take me long, and I don't have to use measuring cups anymore. I'd say both of us have made major improvements. I slide the drink across the bar to him and lean over for a kiss. "It's getting busy, but I'll see you after work?"

"Nothing could keep me away."

Eric mutters, "Please go to his place."

I can't help but laugh and bump into his shoulder.

Coming back to Asheville is the best decision I've made. I've found myself and the person who keeps me from second guessing every decision. He keeps me grounded and keeps the fear at bay.

Almost a year ago, I didn't think I deserved any of this, and now I can't imagine a life without these people in it. I've finally found my home and I'm never leaving it.

acknowledgments

Writing this book has been so much fun., but it's been a beast at the same time. The entire family got sick one right after the other when I was finishing it up. And I want to thank my alphas and editor for being so understanding.

To the family, y'all are amazing and make me laugh every day. You give me so much inspiration. Not only to keep doing what I'm doing, but as I look at characters and how they would react to situations.

My Patrons, Cindy and Stephanie, thank you for your support every month. You have no idea how much it means to me that y'all believe in me enough to support me through it all.

Finally, bloggers and readers. Y'all are the MVPs. Thank you for taking a chance on my books and continuing to support me. I can't wait to see y'all at upcoming events!

also by katrina marie

Out of the Ashes

Cocktails & Crushes

Brews & Bartenders

Mai Tais & Mistletoe

Martinis & Musicians

Gin & Good Guys

The Taking Chances Series

Welcome to Your Life

Cruel and Beautiful World

Ways to Go

Remember That Night

My Only Wish is You

From This Moment

Shoot Down the Stars

Love Will Save Your Soul

Take a Chance

Cousins Gone RomCom Series

Gone Country

Gone Steady

Gone Again

Cocky Hero Club

Big Baller

Silverwood Bulldog Series

Baseball & Broadway

about the author

Katrina Marie lives in the Dallas area with her husband, two children, bonus child, grandchild, and two fur babies. She is a lover of all things geeky and nerdy. When she's not writing you can find her at her children's sporting events, or curled up reading a book.

You can find Katrina Marie online in the following places:
Sign up for my newsletter: https://www.subscribepage.com/KatrinaMarieNewsletter
Website: katrinamarieauthor.com

facebook.com/katrinamarieauthor

twitter.com/katmarieauthor

instagram.com/katrinamarieauthor

bookbub.com/profile/katrina-marie

pinterest.com/katrinamarieauthor

tiktok.com/@katrinamarieauthor

patreon.com/katrinamarie